When The White Crane Calls

"The Worry Stones"

Christian Camarena Series: Book One

First Edition

J. Leroy Tucker

Dedication

I am dedicating this book to what appears real that is not, and to what appears not real that is. It is up to the reader to decide. Thanks to Mike Paquette, Struggling Dreamers Production, and Lisa for helping me with this project.

Editing and internal formatting by Ashley Melander at Nyx Publications.

Table of Contents

Prologue

Elaine lived in Momote Village, a fair-sized housing development and the former living quarters for a military installation shut down as part of the DoD base realignment and closures. Once nice, but now rundown. Jordan Montoya and Christian Camarena lived southeast in Ruskin Heights.

Henry, Christian's uncle, had told him stories of straining to listen, on his Emerson FM/AM pocket transistor radio, to the Dallas Cowboys play on FEN. This was back when he was an enlisted swine in the Army overseas in Vietnam, some time ago. Seemed like yesterday.

A fan of his uncle, Christian became a fan of the Cowboys, and he convinced his best friend, Jordan, to join the club.

This meeting with Elaine wasn't the first. Jordan repeated often to Christian of how he marveled at Elaine during the girls' fast-pitch softball competitions. He went to the games specifically to watch her play. Christian, always the idea person, pushing from behind, was the moral support.

Talented, Elaine played pitcher, catcher, and shortstop. She was also an excellent volleyball player. Jordan and Christian watched those matches too.

Elaine was the only girl who could have made the cheerleading squad and had her own catcher's equipment, characteristics too alluring for the average high school kid. Jordan was no exception. That's how it went, not how it started.

They had been looking for her when Christian saw Elaine first, off in the distance. He tapped Jordan on the shoulder, who veered his gold Triumph in her direction. Jordan's Ray-bans were not enough to prevent the cold wind from jabbing tiny icicle razor blades into his face as he cruised with Christian straddled on the back. The warmth against their legs, coming off the V-twin engine, was not enough to completely abate the cold.

Elaine, standing at the bus stop, hugging herself against the chill, stood apart from the chit-chatting "girlie" girls.

A contrast to the nearly identical heavy makeup, dark eyelashes, laboriously styled big hairdos and orange blush, turtlenecks, and faux-fur ensembles, Elaine's jeans and string-strap crop-cut top afforded little protection against the elements but were a protest against the approaching decade.

Jordan pulled up in front of Elaine. He upshifted to neutral and, without killing the motor, unsure of the next move, removed his letterman jacket and tossed it to her.

Those who wore letter jackets were bestowed status, uplifted and envied by others. Elaine, surprised, almost dropped it. She started to say,

"Hey!" but Jordan did not hear her over the rumble of the engine as he sped off.

As the Triumph motorcycle peeled away, she saw Christian on the back turn, smile, and give her a thumbs up.

Elaine watched as the two rode off down the main drag, uncertain of what to make of the gesture. Was Jordan being gallant, protecting her from the cold? Or something else?

She knew the envy and adoration, even if temporary, were well worth walking the halls the next day in Jordan's jacket. Maybe it was Jordan's warmth and sincerity — or just the simple reality of adding another layer of clothing to her freezing torso — whatever the case, Elaine noticed her shivering had stopped.

Thinking about having to return the jacket reminded her of the time she saw Aunt Naomi sobbing at the kitchen table, explaining to Bachan why she had to give back the engagement ring. *Same here. Jordan will come for his jacket*, she thought. *I'll give it back. But without the drama.* But until then, only the chosen were adorned with the coveted varsity letterman jacket, and she was chosen.

As the bus stopped, Elaine boarded. Scanning for an empty seat, she saw the seated have-nots' heads rise, as if to acknowledge the arrival of their new queen. In their glances, she detected instant recognition of her newfound status. And by the tilting of their heads and whispers, Elaine had instantly become the talk of the village.

Jordan held up a closed fist over his right shoulder. Christian, riding shotgun, open-palm tapped it, acknowledging the fist-bump.

"You were right," Jordan said, teeth chattering. "That worked great."

"You think it would have been better just to ask her to go steady with you?" Christian said over the roar of the engine.

"No, this was good."

He and Christian first met on the Little League baseball field and had been friends ever since. Jordan liked Christian from the start. He liked his folks too, especially Christian's mom.

On opening day, Christian's mom had greeted Jordan in Russian. "Kak dyLAH, vsyo hara SHOH?"

As she shook his hand, Jordan stood dumbfounded.

"How are you? Everything okay?" Christian translated.

"What is that?" Jordan whispered.

"Russian."

Jordan felt like saying, "Is your mom one of those sexy Russian spies who gets info by having sex with her enemies?"

Instead, after Christian's parents sat down in the bleachers, Jordan turned his attention back to Christian and said, "Is your mom Russian?"

"No, American. She learned it at university. She knows Korean too."

"Man, your mom is hot!"

"My mom met my dad in Peru. She travels a lot," Christian explained to Jordan once — after a kid in school, noticing Christian's bi-racial features, asked Christian, "What are you?"

Later, Christian gave Jordan his full family history. "My grandmother on my dad's side, Chiruei, comes from Yamagawa Village in Okinawa, but her family moved to Peru before the war. She married my grandfather.

4

That's why my last name is Camarena. Her name before she married was Yonamine. She came from a family of martial artists whose lineage goes back to the Shuri castle. Her ancestor was Shihan Yaku and bodyguard to King Sho Ko."

But it was a family history Jordan wasn't much interested in at the time. He was still pissed at what Christian had done to him at their second baseball game.

Just as Jordan was shaking Christian's mom's hand for the second time, Christian blurted out, "Mom, Jordan thinks you're hot."

At the third game, Jordan embarrassedly waved hello from afar.

But all was good again after Christian bribed him with one of the crystal worry stones his mother had brought back from Tibet.

"Keep it with you. It's a touchstone. You rub it with your thumb when you feel anxiety or worry," Christian said, relaying his mother's instructions to Jordan.

Elaine did not miss an opportunity to wear Jordan's jacket. She wore it while sitting in the stands, watching their high school games, and if the weather was too warm, she carried it in her arms like a security blanket.

She had accepted his blue and gold-sleeved letter jacket and promised to give it back if either ever decided to break off their high school romance. Jordan had no intention of asking for it back. Besides, she looked so cute in it.

Many envied Elaine, but Jordan knew he was the fortunate one. His fellow teammates liked her, but she had picked him. They didn't just go out. They hung out.

Jordan's dad had few rules back then — be on time for school and come straight home after baseball practice. He did good with the first one, but not so much the second. On occasion, he had to be reminded by his dad smacking him upside the head. But he could accept the punishment if it meant spending a little more time with Elaine.

There were only two passions that took him away from her: when he and Christian were on the ballfield and when Jordan was racing slot cars.

Jordan learned to love racing miniature cars as a little kid when his dad spent time in the Navy as a corpsman. His first experience with slot cars was at the big Army hospital in Bethesda, Maryland.

Back then, it was hard not to notice all those soldiers in blue bathrobes, all bandaged up. They all had their heads wrapped in white gauze or had bandaged limbs and walked around with crutches. Some were missing a leg or arm. Some were being pushed by a nurse. All the robes had the white letters U.S.N. on the front pockets.

But he learned quickly that the guys in the bathrobes built fast cars. Immediately obsessed, Jordan headed straight to the hobby shop located close to Walter Reed, but it was tough trying to keep up with them on the slot car track. Sometimes the soldiers, while racing their cars, if in the right mood, would talk to each other about the war.

Jordan's dad eventually discharged from the military and took a job as an RN in Kansas City, where Jordan, Christian, and Elaine became friends.

Jordan shared his passion for baseball with Elaine but, too embarrassed, never disclosed his love for tiny race cars. He did share Christian's idea about becoming Navy Seals.

"What did you tell him?" Elaine asked.

"I told him no because I can't swim that good — plus, sharks. If we do go, it's the Army."

Elaine and Jordan tested limits, playing around with the concept of love. They went steady, innocently, all throughout high school. His old man noticed their closeness and offered Jordan the condoms in his sock drawer.

Curiosity getting the best of him, one night, when no one was around, Jordan counted six packages. At sixteen years old, most of their peers had experience with sex, but not them. Jordan's mind conjured the notion of filling the condoms with water and using them as water balloons.

Jordan and Elaine were inseparable; she understood him, knew his thoughts. She and Jordan saw the good in people — to the point of being naïve.

"There is good in all people. You just have to look closely," Elaine said.

At that age, he had no life experiences yet to measure against her instincts, but he assumed she was right. She usually was.

While many of their classmates were dealing with adult decisions like teenage pregnancy, drug addiction, and dimly lit tunnels of opportunity, they spent their time catching and returning baseballs he threw her way. Curve, fastball, slider — his best and hardest stuff — no problem, she could handle it, and she could handle him. They had no way of knowing that life was about to throw them some pitches neither one would be able to handle.

———————————————————————

The day she went away came with little warning. He never really understood the full picture. After the divorce, there was talk about Elaine's mom not being able to care for her. He still remembered vividly that day Elaine came to him in tears and said, "I have to move, go live with my grandparents."

"Why?" Jordan said. "Did I do something?"

"Jordan, life is not always about you," Elaine said.

Seeing that she had hurt his feelings, she offered, as a goodbye concession, an opportunity for Jordan to retrieve one of the packets from the sock drawer. Instead, Jordan gave her the worry stone he'd gotten from Christian.

Initially, there were letters from California. Eventually, they became sporadic and then stopped altogether. It was only a matter of time before they lost track of each other.

Jordan enrolled at a local junior college, while Christian tried out for the Fargo-Moorhead RedHawks — an independent minor league baseball club in the American Association. But neither prospect looked promising enough to net the results they both hoped for.

During one return trip back home, Christian said, "I'm going into the Army."

"Ok, me too," was all the thought that went into Jordan's decision.

Planning took as long as they needed to finish chocolate shakes and burgers.

They enlisted in the Army on the buddy plan. Jordan, at eighteen years old, could not imagine life wasn't going to just stand still for him while he and Christian were off playing soldier. He never asked Elaine for his jacket back.

Chapter One

Jordan, seated in the barber chair, his head shaved, on sensory overload, looked into the mirror and saw Christian in the next chair over. He gave him a wink. He appeared joyful.

"Next! Keep it moving!"

"Hoorah, Drill Sergeant!" both yelled simultaneously at the top of their lungs.

Jordan's first taste of military reality was when their plan to stay together after boot camp fell apart. Plans have one universal truth to them: they never go as planned. The Army kept its promise, offering them both a discharge.

Christian, not surprised, told Jordan, "Time to take a bite out of the shit sandwich. You can get out if you want. I'm staying."

Christian, with his ROTC time in high school, number one top recruit status, and high aptitude scores, graduated boot camp as an E-3. While Christian liked being Jordan's sidekick, Jordan knew Christian was the talented one.

After all, he spoke Korean, Spanish, and Russian in high school and was always helping Jordan with algebra. Even when the chips were down, Christian stepped up and did the heavy lifting.

For 20 weeks, Jordan trained at Fort Leonard Wood, Missouri, at the Military Police Training Facility. After finishing M.P. school, he was sent to the United States Army Criminal Investigation Command (CID).

He enjoyed all the trees and woods during his daily runs around the base. He and Christian stayed in touch while Christian was at Fort Bragg with the 75th Rangers.

Jordan and Christian talked about the Rangers. The failure rates were pretty high, and on the off-chance Jordan did not make it, he would have to stay in for two extra years. At the time, he wasn't willing to take the chance.

More and more with passing, Christian seemed less able to tell Jordan where he was headed or what he was doing in the Army (although Jordan did notice that his Korean and Russian had much improved), so the conversation always went back to baseball.

Jordan was not happy with his first assignment and made it obvious. His job — "to provide protection for the Joint Chiefs of Staff, Secretary of the Army, and other dignitaries, as assigned" — sucked, he'd complain.

He did not care much for being what he called a "hey-boy" for all the big-wigs. "An administrative office suck-ass clone," he'd tell Christian over their phone conversations.

He was trained to be a soldier, not a fetching boy for some big-wig's wife's laundry. He grew sick and tired of sitting outside the door of some hotshot, trying not to listen in.

Jordan didn't care about what went on behind closed doors. He figured everyone had a talent and should utilize it the best way they could. He was just bored to death guarding dignitaries and felt his talents were being wasted.

Jordan's boss, Chief Warrant Officer Hargrove, liked Jordan and had filled his head with war stories and acts of bravery. He talked about the "pucker-factor" — of being so afraid that one's asshole squeezed shut and ceased to function, of being in "the shit" and surviving.

"It's strange how the brain knows when the body is getting involved in a potentially dangerous situation and instinctively begins diverting blood from non-vital body parts to vital parts," Hargrove said. "A protection mechanism, the brain knows instinctively to protect essential organs.

Jordan had learned all this from Hargrove during the many conversations they'd had over beers. He wanted to know what it was like, the adrenaline high.

He wanted action and continued to complain about his job until his first enlistment was coming to an end.

"Soldier, you want out of here. Either reenlist or get the hell out — those are your choices. Shitting in one hand and wishing in the other ain't going to make it happen," said the first sergeant.

Jordan wanted out and, as part of his reenlistment contract, received the transfer.

Hargrove always told him, "Be careful what you wish for, boy. You might just get it."

Before shipping out, he remembered Hargrove's last words. "When you take fire, don't worry about shitting your pants. Everybody shits their pants. You can take that to the bank."

Jordan was transferred to the 10th Mountain Division at Fort Drum, New York. When he arrived, a thunderstorm, showers, and winds out of the southwest welcomed him to his new home. He hit the ground running, studying and preparing. He knew that the 10th Mountain Division had a reputation of being one of the most deployed in the Army, and Jordan was chomping at the bit to be a part of the action.

When not involved in training, to acclimate further, he hiked the terrain, spent days in the wilderness, and fished in the Black River that emptied into Lake Ontario nearby. He was determined to be ready when the time came for him to go. Jordan would soon get what he asked for: Somalia.

Jordan's first kill came under the scorching sun while he was sweating in the turret of his HMMWV. He saw the Somali fighter, the achromatic of his skin black against the sun-dried coral stone. The fighter stepped in front of a wall — his fatal mistake. As he stepped forward and pointed an RPG at the vehicle passing in front of him, Jordan, without thought, engaged the fighter with 7.62 X51mm NATO cartridges from the M60.

The fighter, hit, slumped in agony, pressing the trigger while he fell, sending the rocket into the air where it detonated three football fields high. As the convoy continued, Jordan kicked away the M13 links on the floor of the turret from the disintegrating belt of the machine gun.

"Man, one second I'm sweating my ass off, and the next, I'm shaking and feel like I'm freezing," he would later tell Hargrove. "But I've never shit my pants."

Hargrove had said it often, "Look death in the face and kiss death on the lips."

The next time was when he and 8,600 troops, all part of the biggest air assault since Jimmy Doolittle's Raid, were hunkered down waiting for further orders. The soldiers of the 10th Mountain were ready to move out.

They were in Haiti to provide security for Jean Bertrand Aristide, the former priest turned politician, to secure the Port au Prince International Airport, and to re-establish democratic elections.

A sergeant now, Jordan Montoya's squad was assigned to secure Fort Dimanche, the oldest prison in Haiti.

Intelligence information reports stated seeing groups of individuals out of uniform, in civilian attire, still looking uniform. It wasn't hard to put a finger on them if you knew what you were looking for.

They were no different than their American and European counterparts, who, in 5-11 cargo pants, Oakley glasses, and full beards, with concealed weapons sticking out from under their shirts, failed to blend in with the indigenous poor.

No, the Cuban operators were no different. They, too, had a look that screamed, "You don't have ancestors buried in the cemeteries of this town."

As Jordan and his squad walked to their intended destination, they saw barrels filled with torched and burning documents, looters carrying off anything not nailed down, and looks of fear and uncertainty on the faces of children. Jordan tossed one kid a Power Bar.

Intelligence showed that the Cubans, in their withdrawal, were executing political opposition leaders locked in prison cells. Jordan's mission was to confirm or deny the allegations. If the intelligence proved factual, they were to assess and report back to their battalion. Not to engage unless necessary.

The young soldiers had been prepared and anticipated the situation in Haiti coming to a head for a long time. Bravo squad was ready with M-26 fragmentation grenades and an Army-issue M-16 automatic weapon. The weapon was an awesome one, able to fire 700-900 rounds of 5.56-mm bullets per minute. Others carried the M-8 White Phosphorus grenade, which emitted particles of white phosphorus that burned through the skin of its victims. Also carried with Bravo squad was the 40-mm M-70 grenade launcher, able to fire five rounds per minute of CS gas or a variety of grenades up to 300 yards away.

The young soldiers were about to have their questions of bravery, courage, and fear answered for them.

Before moving out, Jordan, now the "old salt," rallied his squad to close ranks to hear over the din of noise. "Forget all that hocus-pocus BS about being a man. Do what you were trained to do. If you mess your pants, so what? I messed my pants the first time," he lied. "So what? Move out."

It felt good to be moving. The squad received its orders to move after having taken advantage of breakfast. He was grateful for the powdered eggs, "shit on a shingle," and coffee. Hell of a lot better than the M.R.E.s he'd gotten used to eating during all those training sessions and forward deployments.

The squad spent the day "humping" their way up the craggy slope as they cautiously approached the outer perimeter of Fort Dimanche. They saw the old French-style stone structure, shaped in giant masonry blocks, covered with a green, slimy, wet moss.

The prison had been erected in 1804, the same year Haiti first gained its independence under the leadership of the former slave Jean-Jacques

Dessalines. It was famous thanks to the dictator Jean Claude Duvalier, who had made it the hub for all torture and executions. Now it was cold, drafty, and had a stale, damp odor unfamiliar to the young soldiers. Jordan knew the smell; it was the odor of death in need of cleansing.

Jordan sighed. He couldn't imagine anyone having to live in such degradation and squalor, jailed or not. The dampness and filth were disturbing. He thought back to his childhood of three meals a day, step-ball games, allowance, mowing the lawn, and hanging out at the deli.

"Thank you, God," he whispered as he looked up at the gorgeous blue sky.

As Jordan and his squad walked the outer corridors, he felt his boots crunching down on inches of thick black ash. He sighed again upon closer inspection, observing that what he initially thought to be soot was moving and skittering along the floor.

Jordan gestured the "shut-the-fuck-up" order to Smitty, one member of his squad, as the soldier almost broke the silence with an expletive remark concerning the size of the cockroaches in Haiti.

Jordan, less flustered, thought the dampness and filth a far better alternative to being shot like a dog while locked helplessly in a prison cell. But then again, nothing was proven yet, and the squad still had a way to go to check out the prison and confirm or deny the information they'd been given.

The squad passed a large, reinforced entrance, which led to a corridor, and entered the prison's inner courtyard. Jordan signaled his squad to split up. Each man, knowing his job, proceeded two-by-two to check out the empty rooms facing into the courtyard.

They reached what appeared to be the main entrance into the interior of the prison, which proceeded downward into a darkened hallway with beams of sunlight escaping through cracks in the walls. The iron-barred gates were rusted open. This was the path to the prison holding tanks.

No soldier complained when Jordan ordered them to dump their 60-pound rucksacks filled with personal and team gear. They would have to duck-walk along the wall about halfway down that corridor and didn't need the added weight.

But before they could advance, each man froze at the echo of small arms fire as it reverberated off the old dungeon walls.

Jordan signaled for his men to remain at their positions while he went ahead to check out what was going on around the hallway corner. The hallway turned at a right angle, and without sticking his head around the corner, he saw the reflections of a flickering light.

Squatting at the junction of the hall, he heard it clearly. The popping sound of a handgun. He knew from experience the pop of a pistol and the thump of a rifle. At first, Jordan was slightly disoriented, unsure of the point of origin. The configuration of the corridors and many chambers distorted the sound, and it seemed to be coming from everywhere at the same time.

While buried in his own thoughts, seconds ticked by. The third gunshot revived him, precipitating a series of panicked screams and yells in a language unfamiliar to Jordan.

Corporal Perez, a native New Yorker and former Golden Glove boxer, whose too many punches to the head gave him an over-stimulated attraction toward violence, crawled to Jordan's position. "The shit is hitting the fan, Sarge," he said.

Perez was sure that the screams were coming from the prisoners as they tried to warn each other of impending death from the pistol-wielding assassin. With each gunshot, they heard booted footsteps walk further down the corridor, followed soon after by another gun blast.

The corporal crouched next to his squad leader, hunched there with a weird little boy look of apprehension on his face, and pulled from his breast pocket a long crochet needle he'd been shielding, brought with him from stateside.

While most eighteen-year-old wholesome young males read "hot car" or "nudie cutie" magazines and fantasized about late-night romps in the back seat, Perez's library collection consisted of books and magazines that researched the art of poisoning human beings with the use of common household products and the "dynamics of death" — how to kill with no immediate evidence of violence. He got his hands on castor beans back in New York when somebody told him they could be used to poison with no trace. He tried to grow some, but he over-watered the plant, and it died.

His plan was to use them on the neighborhood bully, who later became the same real estate agent that hooked up Perez's sister, Maureen. He gave her a break on his commission when she finally bought her apartment off Greystone Avenue, down the street from Manhattan College.

Jordan had seen the needle before. Fourteen hours earlier, they'd sat side by side on the canvas netting jump seats, aboard the inbound CH-47 transport.

Perez had shouted over the prop noise, "Say, Sarge, I read someplace that if you stick a guy right behind the ear with a needle, in the soft spot," Perez pointed at Jordan's ear, "just near the ear lobe, you can kill them. 'Cuz the needle goes right to the brain. It kinda scrambles it up, eh!"

Jordan gave Perez a tentative look. Perez, in his New York accent, continued, "You den take a liddle superglue and dab it over da hole. That way, no blood comes outta the injection site, leaving no evidence." He smiled and offered to let Jordan hold his needle.

Jordan had heard this scheme from Perez before and knew the first time he heard it that the story was crap. Perez believed it, of course, and just didn't bother to research the information further. But Jordan checked on the feasibility.

"The entire brain is encased in bone, dude," a corpsman poker buddy had told him. "The needle won't penetrate the skull, man. Nice try."

Now, even without Perez's insistence, Jordan already knew that, around the corner and down the hall, people were dying.

Jordan looked at Perez and thought, *I'm not about to let your dumb ass go after some dude holding a semi-automatic pistol with a fucking crochet needle.* "Perez, put that shit away before I shove it up your ass," Jordan said.

To Jordan, this was leadership. Keeping ignorance from doing something stupid that would get someone killed.

Jordan took a deep breath, paused for a second, then took a quick sneak peek around the corner.

A Cuban soldier, his face all but indistinguishable. Only a silhouette in the dim light of the hallway. The figure was pointing a small caliber pistol into a cell. He fired once, then turned away from Jordan before walking to the next cell in the line.

Jordan quickly snatched his head back around the corner. *Fuck, he saw me!* His stomach went into knots, and a bead of sweat rolled from his armpit down his side. *Don't shit yourself.*

Jordan was well aware of the paralyzing effects of fear, panic, and terror. His training had taught him to overcome those feelings.

He remembered his Ranger instructor, two inches away from his face, yelling at the top of his lungs, "Pain is just weakness leaving the body! Get it right, or get out!"

Training or no, sweat was rolling down Jordan's face, making his eyes burn, and his heart felt like it wanted to jump out of his chest. *What if I'm wrong? Well, too late now.* He wiped the sweat from his face and negative thoughts from his mind. The Cuban soldier continued down the passageway, unaware he was being scrutinized.

Jordan calculated that the soldier was an officer by the weapon he carried, although he was dressed in a manner that said otherwise. Jordan made his decision. He'd have to take this guy out — quick. Easily said, logistically hard.

He tried to step quietly from his place of advantage, but all the Army-issued gear he wore made the task an impossible one. Jordan stepped silently as he could, which to him sounded as loud as pots and pans hitting the floor at the afternoon chow hall.

The Cuban had already moved down the cellblock. Uncertainty creeping in, Jordan squeezed his eyes shut, opened them, and pressed forward. He heel-toe walked further down the corridor. As he turned the corner, slicing it inch-by-inch, Jordan saw the soldier as the soldier saw him.

The last image Jordan remembered seeing was the Cuban turning with a grim look of surprise and pointing his pistol.

Jordan's finger squeezed the trigger, and his AR-15 recoiled. The sound was overwhelmingly loud. Jordan saw the rounds hit center mass, ripping through the soldier's chest. The Cuban staggered back and slumped to the floor against the wall.

The feeling of someone slapping on the top of his helmet and shoulders woke Jordan from shock. At first, he had difficulty hearing what Perez was yelling. It took a minute for the ringing in his ears to subside. This time, he had only squeezed off five rounds. This time, it was different, more controlled. He still didn't shit his pants.

His thoughts flashed back to his childhood, playing Army as a little kid in his backyard, which sloped down a long, gradual hill into a wooded area. He and Christian, sticks in hand, imaginary guns, shooting and killing each other several times in one skirmish.

"Bang, you're dead."

"No, you missed me."

"No, I didn't. I killed you while you weren't looking."

This time was easier. Jordan blinked a few times. The dead man gurgled, and blood seeped out of three or four holes in his body where the bullets had torn apart his vital organs. They left him where he fell. They didn't bother to check for a pulse. Jordan knew the soldier would die. The Cuban took a final breath and was gone.

No longer a proud officer whose father had been a military officer before him and his grandfather a hero in Castro's revolutionary army. Now a casualty with eyes locked open, staring into infinity. Just dead. His brain had not done its job of protecting all those vital organs.

The prisoners cheered at the sight of the Americans.

Perez stood with his hand in the air, waiting for a high-five. "You gonna leave me hanging?"

Jordan ignored the celebratory gesture. Good, bad, or indifferent, he didn't believe that killing another human being was cause for celebration. His granddad, a carpenter, never celebrated pounding nails. For over 40 years, he didn't boast about his achievements. If the nail stuck up, pound it down. Why? Because it was the right thing to do. Nothing personal.

The squad cautiously moved on. The Army had not ordered them to free the prisoners.

As the squad pushed to the rendezvous point, Jordan reflected on what he'd just been a part of. He had seen the movie *Patton* and immediately idolized the man. He read extensively about him and could quote the general from memory.

"There is only one tactical principle which is not subject to change. It is to use the means at hand to inflict the maximum wounds, death, and destruction on the enemy in the minimum amount of time."

He held back the rush of adrenaline, knowing he'd just gone one-on-one with another human being again and had come out on top. He had faced danger and stood up to it. He had just killed again. He couldn't wait to hook up with Hargrove back stateside and share the news.

As they hoofed it back, Jordan wondered what was for dinner. *Weird that after shooting people, you think of food,* he thought. He'd already missed lunch.

Chapter Two

Jordan sat on a wooden cargo box under the dilapidated awning, dodging the rain as it found its way through. The loud and clamorous roar of the flight line couldn't break his concentration. The C-130s parked on the tarmac, waiting to devour their human cargo. The coup at its end, the soldiers were impatient to get back stateside. Oblivious to the sound of turboprops and GI's shout-talking over the din, he was too busy shoving the Army MRE chili con carne into his mouth to notice.

"Hey asshole, how's it going?" Jordan heard a familiar voice shout over his shoulder.

The rain drenching Christian's cap poured over his face like he was wearing a niqab veil made of water.

Jordan immediately recognized him, even with the slight beard. "Out of uniform aren't you, sir?"

"Got a shaving waiver and the okay to grub down," Christian replied. "Besides, this is my uniform."

"You want to get out of the rain?" Jordan scooted over to give Christian part of the dry spot.

Christian didn't move. "I'm good." The drenching seemed to have no effect on him.

"Christian, you look bigger." Jordan looked down at his MRE. "What the fuck they feeding you guys?"

Jordan hated being wet and cold. He didn't mind wet, and he didn't mind cold. Just hated wet and cold at the same time.

"Sit your ass down, sir," Jordan said. "What the fuck are you doing here?"

Without providing specifics, Christian said, "Keeping an eye on you, as usual. I found out you were on my side of the world, so I came to visit. Good job up at Dimanche. Heard your platoon kicked some ass."

"How'd you hear about that?" Jordan asked.

"Oh, I hear about everything. I get paid to know," said Christian.

Jordan knew Christian could not divulge too much about his reason for being in Central America, and he knew better than to ask but did anyway. "What about you?"

"Another JCET thing. Joint Combined Exchange Training for the natives," Christian said, winking at Jordan.

Jordan figured the JCET thing was a cover for Christian and the 8th Special Forces Group and whatever they were doing down there for real. Jordan, lacking a high enough security clearance, didn't have a need to know.

Changing the subject, Jordan asked, "How are you doing, bro? How's your mom?"

"You're still scheming to have sex with my mom, aren't you? Stop begging."

They both laughed.

Jordan felt fortunate just to have a chance to meet up again with Christian. Sometimes Christian could say more, but most of the time, he could only give vague, elusive answers. Jordan usually figured it best not to ask. He didn't want Christian to feel pressured into saying something that could get them both in hot water.

But he did joke with Christian when he knew no one was listening. "Hey, Christian, wherever you go, crap happens. Uprisings, governments getting overthrown, people getting blown up," Jordan would say.

"Secret squirrel stuff," Christian would laugh.

As they were shooting the breeze, two individuals approached. One was a large, tanned male with a dark beard, and the second, a tall female — Asian, exotic, looked like she could handle herself.

Christian, his back to the approaching pair, caught Jordan's glimpse as they got closer. "Hey, Jordan, these are some of the peeps," he said. "This is my best friend, Jordan. One hell of a baseball player. He should have been a pro," Christian said, hyping up Jordan to the members of his team.

Christian was the guy who never talked himself up. He found genuine joy in uplifting others. Although he was every bit as good a baseball player as Jordan had once been, and in many ways superior, he chose to brag about his friend instead. For some unknown reason, with Jordan, he was content to play the role of wingman.

Jordan fist-bumped them without standing.

The one wearing a Hawaiian shirt and BDUs said, "Sir, Blackhawks are waiting."

By his mannerisms, Jordan thought, *Australian 1st Commando Regiment.*

Wrong. Christian, rarely missing a thing, jerked his head toward the two soldiers as they headed toward the Blackhawks. "Donovan, he's 1st New Zealand Special Air Service.

"What about the supermodel?" Jordan said.

"Wang, she's Air Force, 24th Special Tactics Squadron." Christian did the "zip it" move across his mouth.

Jordan laughed as Christian dug something from his pocket. He had always speculated that his best friend was a member of Task Force 88 or another similar assignment, a mixture of American and foreign special operators.

Christian looked at Jordan and said, "I guess I'll have to catch up with you later, bro. Got something for you."

"What? Another rock?"

"From my mom? You wish. She's moved on from you."

Retrieving a Shemagh desert Keffiyeh scarf from his pocket, he said, "Remember your wingman. Anytime you need anything, you know how to find me. Panama is beautiful this time of the year. We could have used you at Modelo Prison."

"Then who would they have sent to Dimanche?" Jordan said.

"Good point."

"Yeah, stay safe," Jordan replied. He stood and gave Christian a hug and slap on the back. He always felt sadness whenever he had to say goodbye to Christian, knowing that he was always headed in the direction of danger.

As Christian started to walk away, he turned and said, "You decide if you're staying in for another tour when the time comes?"

"Yeah, I decided—"

Christian cut Jordan off in mid-sentence. "Yeah, you're going to make a good cop out there. Besides, it pays a hell of a lot more than in here."

"Here, take this." Christian tossed Jordan his own worry stone he had kept with him since they were teens.

"No, you keep it."

"No, where you're headed, a cop, you're the one who needs it."

Jordan waved at his friend. Christian, seated in the chopper, legs dangling in the rain, gave a one-finger salute as the Blackhawk lifted off the tarmac.

Chapter Three

"Staff Sergeant Montoya, you sure we can't change your mind? You are almost done, sir," Sergeant Major Woolridge said as Jordan signed his discharge papers on the green steel military-issued desk.

He didn't say so, but Jordan had grown tired of the BS — and the spit and polish of a peacetime Army. "Twelve years. I am done, Sergeant Major. Besides, I got places to go and people to see. I plan on staying in uniform, but a different kind of uniform."

The sergeant major shook Jordan's hand on his way out the door. "Good luck to you, son."

At his going away party, he told all who would listen, "The Army only runs well during war. Otherwise, it's a pain in the ass. I'm going back home for a while. See what's up."

Some of the soldiers kept teasing Jordan. "When the civilians get done kicking you in the nuts, don't come crawling back here."

Jordan drove all the way to Cleveland before stopping for a beer and some sleep. The bartender told him the guy just walking out had bought his next beer and told her to thank him for his service.

"Maybe I should grow a mustache," Jordan told the bartender as she handed him the beer.

"No, that won't make any difference. People will always know," she smiled, picking up the tip Jordan had put down.

"Hoorah," Jordan said, finishing off the first beer.

He made it to Kansas City by evening on day two, in a rush to get as far away from Army life as he could. But Jordan was deflated when he got back to Ruskin Heights. Friday night, driving down Blue Ridge, he saw high schoolers and some recent graduates cruising up and down the boulevard. He quickly realized the mistake he had made.

"What did I rush home for?" he asked himself. "There's nothing here for me. These kids are doing exactly the same thing I was doing before I left twelve years ago."

It took months for Jordan to get acclimated to civilian life. Hoorah wiped from his vocabulary, he finally figured out how to act around the civilians, and he accepted the first decent job offered — with the Federal Bureau of Prisons. Not exactly police work, but a start.

Just for now, anyway. No plans on working long in the prison system — he didn't like the proximity to crooks or being associated with them.

"Rub against them too long, you become like them." His words.

Besides, his intention was to become a street cop. "As soon as Kansas City PD starts hiring again, I'm gone," he insisted.

While waiting around for something better to come along, his life became routine. Every weekend, someone was throwing a party. The only difference the years had made: revelers had less hair, and some were chunky. Alcohol wasn't purchased with fake IDs, and babysitter agreements were settled at the end of the night.

Woody, a former high school wrestling teammate, heard Jordan was back in town and invited him. The gnawing irritant after being back — everything was still pretty much like Jordan's mom would say. "Same old, same old."

Woody, now the president of the Ruskin High School Alumni Association, asked, "When's the last time you heard from Christian?"

"I hear from him whenever he's back in the country," Jordan said.

"What's he up to?"

"He's a hard charger, out there kicking ass and taking names." Jordan spoke both with pride and envy about his friend.

"What was that girl's name you dated back in school?"

"Elaine," said Jordan.

"Yeah, that's right," Woody said, staring at his almost empty beer cup. "Yeah, Elaine, you seen her? I heard she was in California somewhere."

"Nah, we kept in touch for a while but lost track of each other. It's been years. She's probably married to some doctor, got kids by now, happy and living the dream," Jordan said.

"Or she could be a fat dumpy housewife or homeless drug addict living on the street," Woody said, recalling some of the girls from their high school graduating class.

"No, definitely not her," Jordan said. "She was always going places."

The last thing I need is to be reminded that Elaine and Christian are out there living their lives while I'm stuck back home guarding crooks, he thought.

People that were worth anything were not satisfied with living in a Podunk town. They did not stick around much. They refused to be absorbed into a life of mediocrity. If you wanted something bad enough, you got it — no matter the time, place, or manner, it got . . . got.

In his travels, he had seen much. He knew he wasn't about to waste what he learned by standing around a keg drinking Coors Lite out of a red plastic cup for the rest of his life. He knew he wasn't staying there long either.

"You need a top off," Woody said, checking on Jordan's beer.

Crumpling the plastic cup and tossing it into a trash bin, Jordan said, "No, I'm done. I'm outta here. Catch you later, Woody. Thanks for the invite."

Before graduation, most seniors didn't have a good feel for life past high school — Jordan and Elaine had been no different. Burning time after school at the steam pipes, the hangout for the local teens, their conversations went along the lines of:

"California, maybe? I don't know."

"Maybe."

"What about college?"

"I don't know!"

One decision where they were of one accord was marriage. Jordan swore she was the only one. Elaine promised to save herself for Jordan. She'd wait for him forever.

Ignorance and naïveté are the catalysts for change.

It was at one of these weekend party repeats where he first met Bellamy. This time, the party was at Williamson's house. Business as usual. Still early, things had already begun to die out. Just the hardcore left standing about getting drunk. Typical. Lots of white T-shirts and jeans, lots of shop talk, booze, and so few available civilian chicks. All the ones there were either sworn or worker bees.

He calculated that this party would no doubt end the same as all the others — a wasted night.

"What the hell? Might as well relax, sip on some whiskey, and watch everyone else get stupid," Jordan said to himself.

No different. Same shit, just a different day, he thought.

He moved away from the table where a group was taking shots. He was much too cautious about the way others perceived him. He wanted to be in control of every situation. Even when affected by alcohol, he tried not to give it away. Personally, he had no patience for people who couldn't hold their liquor.

"I don't mind stupid, and I don't mind weak, but I can't handle stupid and weak together," he often said.

Wanting a drink, Jordan made his way through the kitchen, into the living room, and to the bar. He read the sign that hung on the wall — Williamson's Living Room Bar and Grill. There was a white-faced porcelain figurine of a hobo, red-nosed, leaning against a lamppost. The top of the lamppost was lit, providing a bit of ambient light to mix drinks.

Jordan ignored the cheaper bottles crowding the bar top, instead reaching below where he knew Williamson hid his personal stash, the good stuff. He had come to appreciate Williamson's taste in whiskey.

He took a sip from the double shot he'd poured from the bottle of Henry Dickel Recipe No. 1, scanning the perimeter out of habit until his view came to rest in the center of the room.

There may not be many good-looking women, but at least there's 15-year-old whiskey, he thought. *Although the one with the shrink-to-fit faded jeans, she's not bad. Nice touch, the tears in the knees, and the real tight butt. Kinda slutty.*

Jordan could never figure out the logic. Take a perfectly good pair of thirty-dollar jeans, tear holes in the knees and ass, and there you have it: a hundred-dollar pair of jeans.

She stood in the kitchen, about 5'8", with red hair — not red-orange but red-brown. When he made his initial pass, she was leaning with her back against the sink like a cornered animal, three young guns surrounding her.

Amateurs, stumbling over each other, cock-blocking, thought Jordan.

She was cute; he'd give her that. Maybe worth a try. Possibly. He changed his mind right away after walking back to get a second look. The conversation he heard turned him off.

His target was obsessed with the afterlife. Some metaphysical crap and the existence of other realities. Life force? Jordan took a last look before turning to acquire a secondary target, muttering under his breath, "Geez! Get off the pipe."

But he knew the topic of the conversation didn't matter. Hell, it could have been about garbage disposals or cleaning solvents. She could easily keep those guys' attention — so long as she flashed a smile at them every now and then. Leaving the top two buttons of her shirt unfastened was a definite plus.

"Williamson, what's the story on Tight Jeans?" Jordan pointed with a head nod toward the redhead. "What's her deal?"

Williamson, always the one to have the latest dirt on people, volunteered, "Yeah, she's a cop's ex-wife. Her nickname is Goodhue."

34

"Yeah, like the ambulance service," he said, responding to Jordan's questioning look. "I guess in her younger days, she drove an ambulance. Got fired for giving her future ex-old man extra service while rolling code three."

"Let me guess. There was booze on board?" Jordan asked.

"Does a hundred pounds of dough make a big biscuit?"

Williamson, who was always coming up with what he thought were funny metaphors, continued, "Is a duck's ass water-tight? Does a bear shit —"

"Okay, I get it," Jordan interrupted. "Dude, I want to ride the bike, not learn how to build it."

Half the time, Jordan didn't find much humor in what Williamson was throwing out and didn't believe much of the garbage he spewed, but others thought his comedy genius.

"You going to tap that ass?" Williamson grinned.

Jordan shook his head. "No, dude, not even with your dick." He started to walk away, then turned back, remembering suddenly, "Hey, can I still borrow your truck?"

"You hauling trees again this Christmas? Why do you do that?"

"I want to get a chance to move up in line when I die."

"What line?" Williamson asked.

"The line at the pearly gates," Jordan said. "Besides, if I don't get them something, some of those kids might get nothing."

"Yeah, you got it, just fill it up with gas," Williams said as he handed Jordan a hundred-dollar bill. "Use it for more toys, and hopefully save me a spot in line, will ya'?"

Jordan again started to walk away but stopped at Williamson's nudge.

"I tapped it." Williamson head-nodded toward Goodhue. "It was okay."

Not bothering to notice if Jordan was even listening, Williamson continued, "There I am, going to town, giving it my best effort. I don't mind some conversation while I'm going at it, but she kept wanting to act like a porn star. 'Give it to me, daddy!' Williamson shrugged his shoulders. "I thought I was!"

Jordan reluctantly asked the question Williamson was looking for. "So how was it in the end?"

"Her performance got her on the ghost list. Shit! If I wanted porn, I could get that free on the net. If I have to buy dinner and drinks, I want it honest and with sincerity," Williamson concluded. "Too demanding of my junk."

Jordan gave Williamson a pat on the back and shook his head. "That's because, in your heart, you're a good man," he said, not really knowing what else to say at that point. All Jordan knew was that story was going to cost Williamson another double shot of his finest.

Jordan had a motto: "Never shit where you eat." Always careful about having his business put out on the street. Tight Jeans attracted too much heat. She was a shit magnet.

But then his eyes drifted elsewhere. Jordan saw her for the first time and thought, *She seems like she could be another story*. He caught Williamson's attention, who shrugged both shoulders and mouthed, "I don't know."

She sat at the makeshift dominoes table. She wasn't participating, just an observer. Watching the game and listening to all the trash talk dished out by all the so-called experts.

She was blonde and wore it shoulder length, confident and attractive. By the way she held onto her plastic cup, Jordan could tell it was empty.

Jordan preferred his women that way, a little "thicker" — more like Eva Mendes than the Angelina Jolie type. Watching her brought back memories of that famous Commodores song, "Brick House." Jordan smiled at his recollection of the lyrics.

Jordan watched as the stranger looked up at the clock on the wall. He took the glance as a sign of boredom.

I give her ten more minutes before she makes her exit, he thought. *Need to make my move.*

He was just looking for conversation to help burn some time before going home. But if things went well, he could be convinced to change his mind. The mellowing effect of the Tennessee whiskey was a good start. He was not looking for a wife — only a warm body for the night.

As she scanned the room, he caught her eye. Their fields of vision overlapped and ended with a smile.

She stood up and approached Jordan like she was on a mission. "What are you drinking, soldier?" Waving her hand over his glass as though to take in the aroma.

Jordan, usually attuned to things, didn't catch the reference.

"Fifteen-year-old whiskey."

"You know, I usually never put anything in my mouth that's not at least eighteen years old," she said, smiling at Jordan.

"In that case, let me help you out."

"You have a name?"

"Jordan."

"I'm Bellamy."

He walked her to the bar and the secret stash. "You might like this," he said, offering her a glass. "Ice?"

"Yes, please." Bellamy watched Jordan skillfully start to drop cubes into her glass with the tongs. "Not too many. I like to taste it."

She savored the first sip. "Peppery spice, charred oak, I like it."

My next move is to get her outside and alone, away from the competition, Jordan thought. "Did you know the owner has a koi pond out back?"

It didn't go unnoticed by Bellamy that Jordan spent time in the gym. Earlier, she had observed his deliberate nature as he moved cautiously around the room. She watched Jordan, his head on a swivel, always positioning himself in the best tactical place to see anyone entering or exiting the room. A good sign.

He didn't seem threatening. She'd heard he could be trusted, but she still wasn't seeing the "wow" factor yet.

"Isn't it a little cold?"

"The whiskey should keep you warm enough. If not, we can snuggle."

Bellamy rewarded Jordan with a smile. "Let me get my coat."

"One of the rarest breeds of koi is the Kikokuryu — it has no scales," Jordan told Bellamy as they stood together, looking down into Williamson's beautifully manicured fishpond.

Bellamy had always been interested in other cultures and was genuinely curious about the carp. More so when Jordan explained, "The most expensive koi sold for over 1.3 million dollars."

"Why the hell would someone spend so much money on a fish?" she asked.

"What would you spend it on?" Jordan asked.

"Payback! Debts owed," she said, careful not to give up too much too soon.

Changing the direction of the conversation, Bellamy glanced at the fish swimming in the clear pool. Her eyebrows raised inquisitively as she pointed toward Williamson's pond.

Bellamy laughed when Jordan shook his head back and forth and said, "No, these ain't them."

Jordan figured he had her hooked — not knowing she had him chasing the lure all along.

Jordan had a chance to hone his bullshit mastery during his forward deployment to the Middle East, trips to southeast Asia, and a stint in Europe.

He was a collector of information. He did not view it as a waste of time to spend hours watching history channels or documentaries. He believed information was a way to get to people. Information was power. He knew the right answers, knew the right questions, and knew the right people.

He had learned to play the thousand-question game with any woman to make her feel like she was the only gal in town. Show real interest in whatever she wanted to talk about. Jordan, forever the diplomat, made those who weren't, feel special. He learned that from Christian. Getting more with honey worked. He thought he was testing his skills on Bellamy, failing to realize he was in a job interview.

But his flattery was genuine, and he thought it persuaded her to stay outside much longer than expected. He thought, at least. Overall, a good indication that she was interested in him.

"What brings you to Ruskin Heights?" Jordan asked.

"I'm headed back home from visiting a friend in Cali," Bellamy said. "I owed her a favor. Plus, I needed to prove something to myself."

"I was activated and on the west coast for a while because of all the shit that's been happening," she continued. "The Coast Guard released me from my reserve commitment, so I'm on my way to Iowa to see my mom before going back to California."

"Ever been to Des Moines?" Jordan asked.

"Yes," Bellamy replied. "You?"

"Yeah, I drove through it once. Stopped for gas on the way to Kansas City."

"Then you went through my hometown, Lamoni."

"Yeah, that's right. I remember," Jordan said — while shaking his head no.

"You wouldn't remember a town of 2,000 people," Bellamy laughed. "Why would you?"

"I went to Graceland University," she continued.

Jordan stood watching her, not knowing where she was going with this.

"I'm a good little Mormon girl."

Jordan couldn't mask the look of disappointment on his face. Bellamy, without looking, expected the reaction — she'd seen it before. She remained focused on dropping food to the smaller of the koi.

Bellamy said, "Mom is not happy about me leaving the church. She prays for me to meet a nice LDS guy and have a bunch of babies. But I left town for a reason."

She paused, hesitating. "Dad was too 'loving' and would visit me in the night. Mom knew but didn't give a rat's ass," she continued. "I enlisted a week after the old man got killed. The tractor he was working on tipped over on him. Believe me, I'm going back just to grab the rest of my things."

"I'm sorry to hear about your dad," Jordan said.

"Why?"

Caught a little off guard by her response, he stammered, "Well, uh, you know."

"Oh, yeah . . . I guess you're right. Who would have thought — a farmer and a tractor accident? Karma, I guess."

"Karma?"

"Like how we met today, karma."

Bellamy, feeling comfortable, disclosed, "You know the friend back in Cali? We're best friends. She lived with her mom in a small town around here before moving to California to live with her grandparents. I forget the name. But anyway, we became very close."

Jordan detected something in the way Bellamy said, "VERY close." He wondered, *How close?*

"She's my girl. I love her to death, and we got each other's backs," Bellamy said, as if in answer to Jordan's unasked question.

Jordan was surprised when Bellamy said, "She got out of the Coast Guard and became a cop for a while."

He was pretty sure he had not disclosed to her his interests.

Changing the subject again, Bellamy asked, "Ustaza. You ever heard of it? It's a good place to live."

Jordan shook his head, and Bellamy continued, "I got hired with the city PD there. I start training soon as I get back to California. A well-kept secret, nice and safe. A place where a person can hide and not be bothered."

Jordan, listening intently, nodded his head.

Bellamy leaned against Jordan for warmth and talked. He had to fight the scent of her perfume to stay engaged as details emerged to bind her story and his. He started to feel like he could fill the blank places in Bellamy's recollection with his own story. He recognized a similar pattern between his life and that of the friend Bellamy spoke about.

Jordan wondered. The similarities were becoming matching details. His coming from a small town was the least of it.

Jordan asked Bellamy, "Did your friend play sports?"

"Yeah, she was really good too."

"What sports?"

"Try to guess," Bellamy insisted.

"Softball?"

"Get out of here! How did you know that?"

He knew.

He reminisced about his life in a small town, not trying to be too specific, at the same time fishing for more information. Cruising, field parties, he intentionally kept it vague. Lost in his own thoughts as he recalled the girl he let slip out of his life. The only girl ever to offer unconditional love to him.

It became apparent to one of them that they were both in love with the same girl.

Bellamy confirmed it when she opened her iPhone and showed Jordan her screensaver. It was a photo of Bellamy in a Coast Guard dress uniform, standing next to Elaine at her police academy graduation.

Jordan thought he did well, managing to mask his outward reaction while yelling, *It is her!* No one could hear the shouting — because it was all going on inside his head.

He just couldn't believe it. The woman who still, after all these years, found her way back into his nighttime fantasies, had suddenly become real again. Jordan's heartbeat quickened, and he could feel the adrenaline coursing through his body, fueled by the anticipation of seeing her again. The emotions he felt for Elaine years ago resurfaced.

Different from all the stabbings witnessed while working in the prison, unlike the shootings he had been in while serving in the Army — all emotions he was able to suppress — he felt an overarching sense of regret begin to creep into him. He could not suppress his wish. He wanted so badly to go back in time. He wanted to be back in high school, with nothing having changed. Back when she still wore his jacket.

Jordan wondered how he could possibly see Elaine again. *She's probably married and has kids,* he thought.

As Bellamy placed her phone in her back pocket, Jordan's mind continued to race. He finally said, "Your friend seems very nice," not letting on that he had seen a friendly ghost from the past.

Alone in Williamson's backyard, Bellamy said, "It's getting kinda cold."

Jordan, not feeling the chill, said, "Sorry. Should we go back inside?"

"I have a better idea," she said, taking his hand and walking him to a more secluded area of the yard. She stood looking up at him, waiting for his next move. "I like your snuggling idea better." Not waiting, she moved first and kissed him.

Later, Bellamy invited Jordan to her room for a one-night fling before leaving town. She remembered when Elaine, who was normally upbeat, said something unlike her. "Most people only get one chance in life to make it right. You just gotta go for it sometimes." Elaine was on point.

"I guess every now and then, you just have to take one for the team," Bellamy said.

I wonder how Elaine would take me screwing her high school boyfriend, Bellamy thought. *No, she wouldn't like it. Better that she believes it was an off-chance meeting.*

As she stood in line, plane ticket in hand, waiting to board, her thoughts returned to the previous night with Jordan. She caught herself smiling. She blushed a little, thinking the others in line somehow knew what she was thinking about. Bellamy was happy that she went for it. She got what she came for: insight.

Bellamy wasn't a prude. She enjoyed the thrill of feeling danger and excitement at the same time. She was confident he was the right fit.

Back at her hotel room, he was different. He was attentive and unselfish. She was able to control him, slow him down, relax, and enjoy.

She had accomplished what she'd set out to do. Test loyalty. Hers? His? For her, the end justified the means. For him? It was an opportunity to prove his character.

For Bellamy, it was important to get it right. There had been several full moons since the last time she had been with a man. Appreciating the irony, she thought, *It's like riding a bike. Once you know, you don't forget.* Her only regret was not having more time to thoroughly unravel Jordan.

In the short time she spent with him, she was able to confirm what she already knew. He was predictable — an attribute that made him attractive and alluring to some women. The side benefit was that he was caring in bed — and easy to manipulate. *I can see what Elaine sees in him.*

Bellamy took a chance, hoping he'd take information off her cellphone while she bathed. He could have asked her straight out for Elaine's number, but he didn't, choosing instead to act nonchalant about it. Why? Maybe feeling guilty for having spent time with Bellamy. *He's soft,* Bellamy thought. Whatever the case, she had what she needed.

Early flight, bags packed, Bellamy saw the taxi pulling up through the hotel room window. As she rolled her luggage to the half-opened door, she asked, "Did you get her number?"

She surprised Jordan with the question.

"How did you know?" Jordan replied.

"Why did you pretend you didn't know her?"

"I guess I felt guilty. You're not going to say anything . . ."

"No, we're good," Bellamy said.

"Jordan, before I go, remember when I said Elaine and I were close?"

"Yeah."

"You understand we are together, right? A couple," she lied.

"But . . ."

"Yeah, I know. I like to have options. Elaine, on the other hand, only goes one way," Bellamy said, continuing to weave the fabrication. "So let's keep our little secret between you and me . . . a secret." *Until it benefits me to reveal the truth,* she thought.

Bellamy, not wanting to appear over-eager, decided she would wait until she got home to call and thank him for a great time. Now on the plane back home to Iowa, she reclined her seat and closed her eyes to nap. *Elaine would not like it if she knew I set this up. He's going to come — because she is the perfect bait.*

Chapter Four

The central heating kicked in, and the heat from the ceiling vent woke him. Rubbing his eyes — and then his forehead — he grabbed the half-full water bottle on the nightstand and emptied its contents.

He rolled, half asleep, down onto the floor. "What time is it?" he groaned.

He had said goodbye to Bellamy at the hotel, barely making it home and climbing into bed. His watch now read 2:00 PM.

It took longer to pump out his daily ritual of fifty push-ups and sit-ups. *Payback for a night out*, he thought as he headed into the bathroom. He opened the medicine cabinet, sifted through the different bottles, popped a couple of aspirins, and headed for the shower.

Jordan rested his head on the shower tile as the hot water did its thing, completely immersed under the shower spray, waiting for the aspirins to fully kick in and his head to clear.

Underneath the hot water, letting it drain over him, he stood with a satisfied smirk on his face. He thought back to last night and having to stifle Bellamy to keep them from being heard and getting caught.

Jordan smiled as he recalled Bellamy lying next to him in her hotel room, saying, "I was afraid I couldn't stop myself, even if someone walked into Williamson's backyard and caught us."

Williamson would be proud. Too bad he's never going to hear about it, he thought.

Aspirins starting to kick in and his head beginning to clear, Jordan wondered if Elaine had changed much. Did she still enjoy jokes or being surprised?

As he toweled off, he remembered the time when he and Elaine, Christian, and his girlfriend Mariam had gone to see a horror flick. Afterward, while he and Christian were walking Elaine home, he ran from them, screaming, "Look out! There's something behind you!"

They laughed at her when she just sat down in the middle of the road, covering her head and screaming, "Jordan, I'm gonna have someone kill you for that!"

She laughed out loud in her tomboyish way after finding out Jordan had planned the joke from the start. Jordan paid the price, however — his arm sore from Elaine constantly punching it as they walked.

"The cost of trickery and lies is only retribution and pain," Elaine said.

"Why don't you punch Christian?" Jordan complained.

"Because he's not afraid and didn't run away like you did."

Jordan smiled and unconsciously rubbed his shoulder. His memories of the good old days refreshed. Not thinking Elaine's words were a premonition.

As Jordan dwelled on his past, he grew more obsessed with the idea of meeting Elaine again. For Jordan, it wasn't an issue of want. It was a need to keep his promise to her. It was important.

They were not able to talk at Elaine's home. And like a typical teenager, Jordan couldn't stomach the thought of including his parents in dialog. Instead, choosing to sit across from the deli, spending hours keeping warm on the exposed steam pipes. The ones that came out of the boilers at the shirt factory. She insisted on it, not wanting to go home.

While sitting close during one of those sessions, he pulled out a small box. Elaine opened it to find a silver ring with a single tiny amethyst — all that he could afford on a high schooler's salary. But she didn't care. She put it on her finger and swore never to take it off, promising herself to him.

"I swear to God you will be my first and only," she said.

He promised that he would never leave.

"Do you swear to God you will never leave me?" Elaine asked.

"Yeah, I swear," Jordan responded.

"No! Do you swear to God?" Elaine repeated.

"Yes, I swear to God," Jordan said.

He remembered walking her home — never completely, as he'd always stop in the field across from her house. There, Elaine would extend her arms.

"Nine-second hug," she'd say, holding him in her arms before giving him a kiss goodbye.

He watched her until she went inside her back door. Only then would he get on his motorcycle and ride home.

Elaine's mother didn't allow boys around the house. Jordan had never met her.

Elaine didn't have a dad anymore, didn't know what happened to him. She said that in Algiers he lost an eye and came home a wife-beater and alcoholic. Since then, her mother didn't like men around. It always seemed to upset Elaine to talk about her father, so they tried never to bring him up.

Already dissatisfied with his current situation, meeting Bellamy was the sign he had been waiting for. He was looking for a reason to pull the pin anyway. This was it.

Knowing he had already let one opportunity slip by, he damn sure was not about to blow it a second time.

"Pack your shit. We're out of here," Jordan said to himself.

Chapter Five

She was not hard to find. Her thick, long, dark hair gave her away. It flowed unencumbered down her back, straight, not straightened. *She's still got it,* he thought.

Three days of observation had netted the same results. Her mornings never changed. At the park at the same time as the hardcore joggers and departing before the yoga class. Choosing to sit on the same park bench every day.

From his vantage point, despite all her sameness, he detected change. Maybe it was the tear stains. She sat lost in deep thought, as though in prayer. But her eyes remained open.

At first, he instinctively took several steps toward her, then hesitated, suppressing his desire to rush to her. Waiting for a sign.

As he watched Elaine, he glanced toward the trees. He had a dream last night of a muddy river and knew bad luck was to follow. Not superstitions, but signs.

Elaine, blowing warm breath into her clinched hands, stood up from the bench. Careful not to slip on the red, orange, and brown wet leaves that had fallen and covered much of the footpath, Elaine wandered towards her car. There she stood frozen, somber, keys inches away from the car door lock. Her gaze shifted to the row of pistachio trees. She saw a white bird resting on a branch. She squinted, as if to make sure she was seeing correctly.

Not at all cautious, the large bird dropped out of the tree. It walked the few steps down the path, then stopped and stood near the same bench Elaine had vacated.

Suddenly, wings spread, it flew to the tops of the trees. As the white-naped crane rose, a second bird appeared. Both turned and flew east. She watched them glide past the tree line. Jordan saw a stark change in her. She took a deep breath, stood a bit straighter, and began to climb into her car.

Jordan saw as Elaine watched. White birds or any white animal showing up out of nowhere was definitely a sign of bad things to come.

Jordan decided to approach her, having no idea what to say. He tried to picture some romantic movie where Elaine jumped into his arms, overjoyed to see him.

Elaine looked at Jordan and smiled a little. "I missed you, my friend," she said. "Bellamy said you would come. I always knew you were different. We have a lot of catching up to do." She approached him slowly. "But first," she said, "nine-second hug," and went into his arms.

A green and yellow striped patio awning and dark wood Corrigan studio furniture accented the restaurant's patio. Billy Joel played over the outside speakers, inviting the two friends to sit. Warm enough and more secluded, they talked chronologically through their lives, from high school to now. Stress had etched slight wrinkles in her brow, yet all the while,

Jordan, recollecting Bellamy's departing words at the hotel, searched for a glimpse of the high school girl he still loved from long ago.

A couple holding hands strolled by. Goth. The young girl wore a long trench coat. She was in all black — Doc Martins, hair, nails, eyeshadow, lipstick. It all said, "I need to be respected. I'm invisible, so stay away."

Jordan didn't notice, desiring only to rewind as many of the years with Elaine as possible. Elaine sat looking troubled, somehow different, dark in her mood. She had changed.

Jordan, intently eyeing Elaine, tried to hold her gaze. About to speak, he started to place his hand on top of Elaine's, which rested on the table.

She instinctively pulled back. "I'm sorry."

"That's okay," Jordan said, misunderstanding her intentions. "It's been a long time, I understand. People change."

Elaine lightly touched his fingertips. "Yes, that's true."

Jordan understood police work took something away. The tragedy and sadness associated with the profession always chipped away at an officer's innocence. But this was clearly something else that he couldn't quite comprehend.

"Elaine, who is Bellamy to you?" Jordan pried.

"Why?"

"Well, because I'm not sure about her."

"What's not to be sure? She's my best friend from the Coast Guard," Elaine said.

"Is that it?"

"Is that what?" Elaine asked.

"I mean, is that it?" Jordan insisted.

"Look, she's one of the best, Jordan. A very dear friend."

Not satisfied with Elaine's answer but figuring he wasn't getting anything else, Jordan asked, "How's your mother?"

As Elaine began to recap her past several years, his heart sank deeper. *Stupid asking about her mother so early in the game,* he thought.

"Mom is long gone. I lived with my grandparents until recently." The answer, followed by a look of grief and pain, opened the floodgates, releasing Elaine's tears.

The waitress, about to drop off waters, stopped, fingered her crucifix pendant, went back to the kitchen, took the waters from her tray, and poured them into the sink.

The black shroud of the passing couple paled in comparison to the black cloud that engulfed Jordan. As Elaine shared her life, he grew more distressed for her.

Jordan did not miss the meaning of the white birds he had spotted earlier, and he knew inside, *She isn't done.*

She leaned forward and whispered, "They tried to offer me money." Leaning back in her chair, "I did the right thing.

The waitress returned with pad and pen. "Can I take your drink order?"

"Lite beer."

Elaine said, "Whisky."

"Me too then, only make mine a double."

"Same here."

As the waitress turned and walked away, she pushed the silver bottle opener deeper into her back pocket.

Elaine continued, "I told them I was going to go to the right people. So they sent messages. I should have listened and moved on sooner. Bachan would still be alive. It's my fault. They made it look like an accident."

"What are you saying?"

"I knew what I did would end careers. But my decisions ended lives. They made life unlivable," she explained. "Getting the cold shoulder from other police officers, okay, fine. Working alone with no backup, that sucked. But the worst of it . . ." Elaine paused. "Death threats! Murder! Not coming from the crooks I threw in jail, but from my own people, other cops."

"The family I belonged to turned their backs," she said.

Jordan asked, "Can you prove what you're saying?"

Elaine's eyes jabbed into him. "I am way beyond that, Jordan. I don't need more proof. I need to do what I have to do."

The past year had been a nightmare, and after taking her concerns to her boss, it got worse. Even so, Elaine was still determined not to leave things alone. That's when life really started to become unlivable.

Elaine grew accustomed to removing the remains of dead rats from the front seat of her patrol car and finding disgusting comments and graphic notes in her pigeonhole at work. Eventually, things got to a point where Elaine had a choice to make: quit, be fired, or get hurt.

Elaine was accustomed to being the only female in a predominately "boys" profession. But being left alone at the end of each shift was different and took some getting used to. Usually, people hung back to debrief on the day's events. Not for her. By the time she rolled back into the station, everyone had disappeared.

The evidence locker room was in a detached section of the station. Elaine parked at the far end of the police station parking lot. She climbed out of her patrol car, walked around to the passenger side, and collected several bags of evidence on the passenger side seat in her arms. She struggled to keep a grip on the bags while punching the combination on the door to the evidence locker. She walked inside to book the evidence.

By nature, the storage room was always kept cold and dark, but when the power shut off, it went pitch black. Her first thought was, *Power outage. Emergency generator will kick on, no worries.*

The ringing sound in her ears was deafening, and the flash she saw, bright. The pain was incredible. When the lights went out, she reached for the flashlight hanging from her belt. That was when the punch landed flush on her cheek. Elaine felt the blunt tip of second-growth hickory wood from a police baton. Someone hiding in the dark jammed a police baton into her kidney, then came the second punch to the face.

The force of the stick drove her forward, right into the oncoming punch — which made it worse. She tried to remain in the fight. As she fell back, she reached out blindly, accidentally knocking evidence boxes and envelopes off shelves.

Her instincts were to stay on her feet, fight. "Live or die by your training," she'd been taught. "Cops are like turtles on the ground. Don't go down!"

Just as she put up her guard and focused on the attacker directly in front of her, the fourth and final strike from behind jabbed into her spine. She dropped to one knee.

She felt the coarseness of the bag against her cheeks as it was pulled violently over her face. She tasted blood — her own — as her lip was slammed into her teeth by the hand covering her mouth. She tried to bite through the hand stifling her cry for help. She fought to reach for her duty weapon.

"Oh no you don't, bitch!"

As she was shoved to the ground, someone held her wrists, pinning her arms above her head.

"Hold her legs!"

A body sat on her legs. She struggled against multiple assailants. *How many of you fuckers are there?*

Hands pulled at her utility belt. Her gun was taken and tossed across the room, as was her pepper spray canister.

One started to tear at her uniform top and ripped at her ballistic vest.

She immediately recognized the smell of the cologne he wore, but did not dare say his name, for fear it would result in her death. Determined to disrobe her, he grabbed at her undergarments. Enraged, she fought, but the weight and numbers were too much to overcome. She was able to turn over and get to her stomach.

She wasn't going to let them hear her cry. Crying not like when a hammer smashes on a finger, but more that of the tears that flow at the funeral of a friend. That kind of crying. In her mind, she thought her worst fear was about to come true. She was going to be raped.

Elaine yelled, "Fuckers! You'll have to kill me first!"

Even if it happened, she damn sure wasn't going to let them hear her cry.

"No! We are not doing that!" one of her assailants objected.

The attempt to remove her clothing stopped.

Elaine was caught off guard when she heard the pop and felt two prongs from the taser pierce her lower back — followed by what seemed like 50,000 volts. Her body locked up. It hurt the worst in her joints, between her skull and neck. This time, she collapsed for good.

As suddenly as it had started, the assault ended. The message delivered.

She lay there in her pain, misery, shame, and relief — feeling blessed and guilty at the same time. There was a sense of euphoric relief, having survived the ordeal.

Her attackers rushed out of the room into the dark as quickly as they came, throwing the bolt on the door from the outside. Elaine was locked in.

As she lay on the tile floor, she ripped the bag from her head, and a voice from behind the door whispered into the blackened room, "Snitches get stitches. You should have taken the money, rat. Keep your pie hole shut!"

It felt like it took hours for Elaine to finally find her equipment strewn about and to compose herself. To add to the humiliation, she had to call the dispatcher to ask for someone to come and unlock the door. It was a long night before she finally got home.

Elaine slept with her weapon under her pillow. She requested several days off, not wanting to see the looks on their faces when they saw what they'd done to her.

Eventually, gaining the strength she needed, Elaine requested an exit meeting with the chief.

Elaine stood outside of the police station, her thumb unconsciously rubbing the worry stone inside her pocket. She mustered the courage to go inside. Holding her open palm in front of her mouth, she huffed a breath into her hand, then reached into her pocket for a stick of chewing gum, recusing herself from logic. Her breath should have been the last thing to concern her as she walked into the outer office of Chief Elliott's receptionist.

"The chief will see you, Officer," said the blonde-haired receptionist, who sat ramrod straight in her office chair.

Elaine stood and went for the door emblazoned with "Chief J. Elliott." She suddenly stopped, remembering she still had the gum in her mouth. She looked for the trash can and started to toss the chewed gum into the trash, but she paused, noticing the look she was getting that said, "Oh no you don't."

Elaine, spying a yellow crumpled envelope in the trash, tore off a corner, wrapped her gum in it, and discarded it into the bin — earning a smile from the receptionist.

Funny, that envelope looks familiar. But Elaine was not able to place where she'd seen it before.

She knocked.

"Come in."

Elaine sat waiting for his response.

"I will get to the bottom of this," he said, without looking up.

Somehow, she didn't believe him.

As he spoke, he jotted notes, never looking at her.

"People need to go to prison," Elaine said.

"Well, let's not be too hasty — until we find the facts. You have proof it was Cerna?" the chief asked.

Chief Elliott, a short, chubby intellectual type, much younger than he looked, finally looked up. He rose from his desk and walked to his office door, making sure it was properly closed.

He sat back down behind the large mahogany desk and crossed his arms. This time giving her his full attention. He looked at her, eye to eye.

"I will help in any way you want. But I cannot guarantee that I can protect you," he said.

"You mean you won't protect me is more like it. I can always go to the Feds," Elaine threatened.

"If you do, you'll be blackballed, through being a cop." Chief Elliott acted as though he didn't have a dog in the fight. "You do what you must do. Besides, I'm less than one year from my full pension . . . Perhaps it would be best for you to move on while you still can. It's for your job security and safety. I'll give my full endorsement to anyone who wants to hire you. You have my word."

With that, Chief Elliott stood, indicating the conversation was over, and offered his hand. Elaine turned her back without accepting and walked out of his office. She could feel the heat from the burning bridge on her back.

As she passed the trash can where she had tossed her stale piece of gum, she suddenly recalled where she'd seen that envelope before.

She remembered Cerna tried to give her one when she first started on the job.

"Charlie Brown," Elaine said under her breath as she walked out of the building.

Elaine stood staring into the mirror hanging in the back of her police locker. As she pulled personal belongings out one by one and placed them into a cardboard box, she couldn't help thinking how long it had taken to earn the right to occupy a police locker and how little time it took to empty it.

Unceremoniously, she turned in her uniform, gun, and badge. She knew her life, as she had known it, was finished. It would not take long before word about Elaine leaked.

Whether she went to the Feds or not, no agency would touch her with a ten-foot pole after this. She had become a pariah.

It took a while to make the adjustment. Elaine settled for a regular job and moved back in with her grandfather. She needed to stay in the shadows until things blew over.

Being labeled a snitch, getting a rat jacket, being blackballed was one thing. Assault and the death of her loved one was something else entirely.

"Jordan, you know I'm not exaggerating, right?" She looked at him. "I got my grandmother killed. Life is over for me. I have nothing to lose."

Jordan, who was usually good with words, sat silently, hands folded on his lap, not knowing what to tell the one person he should have words for.

Finally, he said, "Listen, I'm here for you. Whatever I can do to help. I would give my life — that's how strong my feelings are for you." He went on, "I'll help you get a good attorney. But if you are asking me to commit crimes, I'm not doing that."

"I'm not asking you for anything! You are not like them," Elaine said. "Don't worry about me. I have a plan. I can take care of myself."

Later that night, Jordan lay in the hotel bed, his vacation days coming to an end. He had to get back to his new life. But his thoughts were focused on Elaine and what she said in the restaurant earlier. *A plan? What plan?*

He would meet with Elaine one final time before driving back home.

Chapter Six

Officers Rice and Pasteur were seated in their police cars, waiting behind Nguyen's Doughnuts, when Officer Cerna pulled up and stepped out of his with three yellow envelopes in hand.

Cerna was not the type to flip people off from the safety of his car. He was the one who got out of his car and smashed their window.

As he handed each a yellowish beige envelope with a brown stripe, Pasteur said, "Did I ever tell you this looks like the Charlie Brown character's shirt?" pointing at the stripe on the envelope.

"Every time."

Pasteur began to open his.

"Count that shit later, Pastor. How many times I gotta tell you?" Cerna said, looking irritated.

"It's Pasteur, not Pastor. Like Louis Pasteur."

"Whatever! You want to stay on this team, you do what the fuck I say!" Cerna said.

Pasteur looked at Rice, who shrugged his shoulders. "Whatever!"

Rice looked at Cerna, "I was talking to the Rook about the fish caper."

Pasteur was technically no longer a rookie, but had to keep the title until the next new trainee passed probation.

"That's bullshit, man!" Pasteur said, not having any of it. "You're shitting me."

Rice replied, "It's fucking true. I wouldn't shit you. Besides, why would I shit you? You're my favorite turd."

"Get out of here with that! There's no way," Pasteur continued.

"Tell this fool, Cerna," Rice said.

"It's real. We were both there. We both saw it," Cerna said. "The poor shmo was lying face down on the bed with a fishtail sticking out of his ass."

Still not convinced, Pasteur said, "What? The fish swim up his ass while he was in a river?"

"Nope, wrong answer," Rice said, shaking his head and holding back a chuckle.

Pasteur asked, "What kind of fish?"

Not skipping a beat, Cerna replied, "It started out a frozen mackerel when it went upstream. The fins thawed out on its way back. That's how it got stuck."

Pasteur, with a look of disgust, shook his head in disbelief and asked, "How the hell did he end up with a frozen fish up his ass?"

Cerna said, "I guess if you really want to know, you'd have to talk to the dude's wife, the fish whisperer, about that."

Rice laughed and high-fived Cerna.

"Fish whisperer? That was good."

Rice yelled to Pasteur, "If you want to know what it's like so bad, why don't you try it?"

Pasteur walked to his patrol car, popped the trunk, and placed the envelope into his war bag. "Because there's a tattoo on my ass that says 'exit' not 'entrance.' That's why."

Before closing the trunk lid, Pasteur retrieved a brown paper bag containing two prepaid cellphones.

Rice said, "People do some crazy-ass shit when they got nothing but time on their hands. Whatever happened to knitting or crossword puzzles?"

"Is everything locked on?" Cerna called out.

"Yeah, the idiot we recruited should be in the store by now," Rice said.

"How do you know he'll show?" Cerna asked.

"Because he picked up the backpack from where I left it, and he thinks he's getting paid — that's why."

"Cellphone?"

"He got that too. Told him to make a phone call if anything strange happened."

"You know what to do, Pasteur," Cerna said, nodding to him and Rice.

"Yeah, I'll make the calls."

Chapter Seven

As expected, the call came out. Disturbance at Sanada's Hardware. Sanada's store had been a fixture in the thriving immigrant community of Japanese and Japanese-Americans.

That was, until Executive Order 9066 dashed dreams and forced entire families out of Orange County, the Fillmore District, L.A., and the small town of Claypond, relocating them to places like Heart Mountain, Manzanar, and Tule Lake.

The homeless man stood in the aisle, stuffing lithium batteries into his new backpack — hot items for pawn shops. The first anonymous 911 call had reported a shoplifter committing theft inside the store.

As the dispatcher relayed the request for assistance, moments later, a second 911 call came in. The second, another caller wishing to remain anonymous, provided information that a backpack-toting bad guy was in Sanada's store and in possession of a handgun.

The dispatcher released the second transmission. "Officers requested to respond now, code three."

Officers Rice and Cerna nodded at each other and donned black leather gloves — a sign that their beat team was ready to "go to work."

Brake pads smoking from overheating, two units arrived at the same time at the front entrance as the backpack-toting thief exited the same doors. Caught in the confusion, he saw the officers kick open their squad car doors and, with guns drawn, take cover behind the red and amber flashing lights. The thief, looking confused and panicked, shouted, "What the f . . . what the f . . . what the f . . . what the hell is going on?!"

A few seconds later, Officer Pasteur arrived and stepped out, gun drawn. "Get on the ground!"

As Rice and Cerna tactically moved from the protection of their patrol cars to make the arrest, the thief suddenly remembered, *If something strange happens, make the phone call.* He reached into the backpack.

"Don't do it!" came the warnings.

Officers were shouting, "Get on your knees!"

This wasn't the plan, the thief thought. *I need to make that call.*

The store manager, Mrs. Beatrice Mikazaki, whom everyone called Betty, had followed the suspect and started to lock the two doors behind him as he exited. She, too, was equally surprised by the sight of the officers. Store policy was to call the police only after the suspect was long gone. Betty sternly warned all her employees, "Never go outside."

Who called the police? was her last thought.

"He's got a gun!" a call rang out from the direction of the police cars.

The confusion on her face turned to disbelief when the two officers began discharging their weapons — with her and her customers in the direct line of fire. Her body folded at the initial impact.

Had she known it was about to hit the fan, she surely would not have followed him. Her days as an Army nurse back in the war had taught her what bullets can do to a body. Too late for Betty — she was met with a hail of gunfire ricocheting off doors and plowing through store windows.

Officer Rice fired his Smith and Wesson nine-millimeter, followed by the sympathetic response from Cerna and Pasteur's Glock 45s. Bullets disintegrated the glass entrance doors.

One customer dove for the floor. The others panicked and ran from the storefront to escape what they thought was now an active shooter.

Betty retreated into the store to escape the hail of gunfire. The suspect, terrified and confused, dropped his backpack and followed.

Additional Claypond City PD officers responded to what was now being mistakenly called in by several onlookers as an active shooter in the hardware store.

Elaine arrived to chaos and the sound of gunshots. The wind in her face carried smoke and pepper, the smell of burning sulfur, and carbon coming from igniting primers coated in graphite. It was loud, not like the polite banging sound of gunfire on T.V. More like a loud ringing bell that caused her to flinch and duck with every peal.

She felt the energy from shockwaves shatter through her body. She watched the suspect turn and reenter the store.

The officers quickly lined up, formed into a stack, and began to make entry — before being stopped by the incident commander.

Elaine's primary role was that of an officer, but she had to fight back the panic and sick taste rising up in her throat. Not for her own safety, but from fear. The woman she called Bachan, Japanese for grandmother, who had held her crying when Elaine's mom passed away, who soothed her concerns the night before she left for the Coast Guard — she was in there!

Bachan had always been there for Elaine in her time of need, and now Bachan needed her, but Elaine was too far away and of too little help.

"Bachan, please remember what I coached you to do," she prayed. "Hide. Fight. Run."

Elaine's heart sunk to a depth of total despair. Word came over the comms. There were confirmed dead in the store.

Elaine pushed to go in, "My grandma is in there!"

There was no use fighting. She was physically held back by peers whose plans were to stand fast and wait. Soon, the gunfire abated; this was now a barricaded subject situation. Paramedics staged nearby, ready to render aid once the police made the area safe.

Officers, denied entry, remained at their assigned posts until customers and employees slowly began filing out of the building.

Elaine's hopes turned to anguish when customers and employees exiting provided intel that there were multiple confirmed casualties. One was the suspect. A second was a possible customer. The third was the store manager, Elaine's bachan, Betty.

As teams finally began to make entry, Rice and Cerna were the first to discover the suspect, dead from gunshot wounds, and over the radio, they heard additional officers identify a female deceased near the power tools, lying motionless in a pool of blood.

Officers Rice and Cerna looked at each other with an understanding fist bump. Rice scanned the area for possible witnesses, handing Cerna a small-caliber semi-automatic from his jacket pocket. "You know what to do."

Rice took a position to watch for onlookers. Cerna squeezed the handgun into the suspect's palm. He took it, removed the magazine, unloaded the weapon, and placed it in a plastic bag he had in his pocket.

Elaine recognized her bachan on the floor in a pool of blood. Two bullet holes pierced her body — one a direct hit, the other through her right rib cage, as though she'd had her hands raised.

"No, no, no!" Elaine screamed in agony.

Overcome by the intense emotional trauma of seeing her grandmother lying there, she felt a sensation of warmth, nausea, and lightheadedness take over. Her vision closed in and began to gray. An officer standing nearby called to her, his voice sounding as if it was coming from a tunnel. He caught her just before she completely collapsed to the floor.

Elaine vaguely recalled sitting on the bumper of the ambulance, a blanket wrapped around her shoulders, dazed and in shock. What she didn't remember was how she ended up in a hospital bed with Gichan leaning on his cane, standing over her.

She opened her eyes and saw her friend Bellamy dozing in a hospital chair. "How did I get here?"

Bellamy awoke. "You were transported. It's been three days . . . do you remember anything?"

"Yes. How is Bachan?" Elaine asked.

Bellamy, shaking her head, said, "Elaine, I'm so sorry . . . she didn't make it."

Elaine covered her face with a pillow and sobbed.

Officer Rice covered up the publicity nightmare, saying, "I saw a pistol in the suspect's hand, so I fired."

Cerna claimed, "When I heard gunshots, I thought they were coming from the suspect, and to protect Officer Rice, I engaged him with deadly force."

After some coaching, Officer Pasteur confirmed that he thought he had seen the suspect point a black object in the direction of Rice and Cerna.

It took more than a year before the officers were exonerated. Families, of course, hired attorneys, sued, and settled for damages. The agency admitted culpability. The chief of police eventually retired and moved his family to the Lake of the Ozarks. The city paid to hush things.

Elaine's family received no compensation — they asked for none. Elaine's grandfather refused to go after compensation. It wouldn't return Betty. Besides, he thought he could avoid making things worse for Elaine. He was wrong.

Chapter Eight

It took about eight months for the news to come that he had been hired on with Baldwin PD. The town was about an hour's drive from Claypond. Jordan liked it there. The streetlights reminded him of home. It was big enough, without being too big. It had a Ruskin Heights feel to it — without the cheap gas, cheaper rent, and the freezing winters. If he wanted to get lost, it didn't take long to get to the woods. The people were cool hippies who, for the most part, had grown up to become their parents.

Not many were knocking down doors to go into this line of work. They had their minds set. Jordan was a breed of his own. He was meant to drive a black and white car.

Police Officer Jordan Montoya grabbed the cup of hot brew and made sure the lid was tight.

He turned the front doorknob and just missed a scorpion the size of five dimes.

"Ouch!" Jordan said instinctively. "This is going to take some getting used to."

The scorpion, unless it was pumped full of 'roids, was not going to get him, he realized. At first, Jordan just stood there from a safe distance, looking at the beast. He'd heard there were some of these things running around but had never seen one in real life. He ran back in, got an empty mayo jar, and took it prisoner.

Should he take it to the police station? He then thought better of it — what if someone got stung?

"That definitely would make for a bad day," he said, having a face-off with his captive. "People around here live with these things, probably no big deal."

So instead, he left the jar and captive on the porch and took off for work.

His first months as a new guy took some getting used to. Not like he was a real rookie in the truest sense of the word — cop work is cop work, and his strategy had paid off. In his off days back home, he'd worked part-time as a constable, volunteering as a limited-duty police officer. When he was hired, all he needed was a few rides in the police car to figure it out. Besides, relocating wasn't foreign to him. This wasn't the first time Jordan was learning a new environment. He knew the drill. Keep his head down, don't talk too much, answer his calls for service, and handle his own paper.

"No, not really," he said, when asked if he moved to Baldwin because of the money. "I needed to be closer to my girlfriend," he took the liberty of saying. Although Elaine and Jordan were not actually together, and he still wasn't sure if she was even interested in men, he thought it made him seem less like a stalker. "She lives in Claypond."

Chapter Nine

Elaine and Jordan walked along the sidewalk, approaching the home where her grandparents helped raise her. Elaine grabbed Jordan before he stepped onto the grass.

"Don't step on the poopoo," she said, pulling him back onto the sidewalk.

Jordan thought back to high school, remembering Elaine's weird phobia about dog poop landmines hidden in the grass. He liked to tease her relentlessly whenever he found one, holding his foot inches away, threatening to step in it.

It was all fun and games until Jordan convinced Christian to try it once.

"Like this?" Christian said.

"Yeah, put your foot really close, like you mean it."

Jordan snuck up behind as Christian reluctantly hovered his foot over a fresh pile, half-heartedly teasing Elaine.

Jordan, meaning to step on top of Christian's foot, forcing it down into the mush, instead found the tables turned when Christian instinctively moved his foot just as Jordan was about to stomp down on it. The dog poop landmine exploded under Jordan's white Converse All-Stars. If it were a real mine, Jordan would have lost a leg.

Jordan dragged his foot across the grass — amid Elaine's screams and panic. "Oh my God! Jordan!"

He found a twig and tried to scrape the remnants of filth from the crevasses of his shoes as Christian smirked. "Hey, Jordan, my mom told me that I was born at night . . . but not last night."

"Oh no you don't! You're throwing those away," Jordan recalled Elaine yelling at him from twenty feet away.

The neighborhood was old, but the homes were well-kept — like most of the ones Jordan had seen on Flower Street back when he went on a ride-along with the Santa Ana Police Department. Only without the gang problem.

As they were about to enter the house, Elaine reached out and grasped Jordan's bicep. "Before you leave, I want to introduce you to my grandfather."

When they walked in, Elaine called out, knowing not to startle him, "Gichan, it's me."

Jordan scanned the hallway. A mirror hung on the wall. There was a skinny table with a framed photo of Elaine in her police uniform. He saw several kokeshi dolls — all small, except one.

Somewhat of a hobbyist on Japanese culture, Jordan had seen similar dolls before. He recognized the eight-inch tall one and guessed it had been made by Katase Kaihei, an artist whose studio was in Kanagawa Prefecture. It was a vintage Japanese Oboroyo.

A shadow box tucked away in the corner stopped his survey of the house. Mesmerized, he dropped to one knee to take a closer look, wiping the dust from the frame. He recognized the Combat Infantry Badge, Distinguished Service Cross, Silver Star, Bronze Star, and Purple Heart — all combat action medals and ribbons, clustered with bronze and silver oak leaves. He saw the patches of the 100th Infantry Battalion and 442nd Regimental Combat Team.

"Holy moley, Elaine. Your grandpa is a badass."

Jordan knew the stories and recognized a red, white, and blue shoulder sleeve insignia with Lady Liberty holding a torch.

Based on the stories he'd heard and his own experiences, he knew what it took to receive acknowledgments like those represented in this glass box. He felt a small, undeserving connection to its owner.

He bowed his head. He understood why such a hero did not display this significant time in his life in a place of prominence, instead choosing to squirrel it away in a corner of a room. Elaine, sensing Jordan could be there staring for some time, tapped his shoulder. Jordan looked up and met her smile. He carefully placed the now-dusted shadow box back in the corner, stood, and let her lead him into the den.

Jordan saw Elaine's grandfather, Gichan, seated in a worn La-Z-Boy recliner, watching baseball. The man's gaze shifted from Ichiro to Jordan.

Gichan had that gaze reserved only to those who'd "been there and done that." When you saw it, you knew it.

The look of someone who had contributed to a mountain of deaths — and seen even more. He scrutinized Jordan. His gaze held neither anger nor joy.

The den was the final resting place for reminders of a long life, filled with "I'm Sorry for Your Loss" remembrances from a not-so-recent funeral.

Flowers browned, withered, long dead, like a Christmas tree left too long after New Year's, in need of carting off the holiday battlefield.

Vases, arranged in formation, once stood as ramparted sentinels for the young couple. Now petrified urns for dead flowers and condolences.

The room, once alive, was destined to remain stuck in time, like the vintage World War II studio photograph of a young Nisei girl and her handsome soldier boy.

Beatrice's brother, Shigeo, had introduced her to Harold, Elaine's gichan, while the two soldiers were on a visit to the Jerome relocation center where Beatrice and her family lived.

Before shipping out for Italy, the Buddhaheads from Hawaii and kotonks from stateside were not coming together as a fighting unit. So the groups were invited to internment camps to meet girls, dine, and dance.

Harold told Elaine that, when he saw Beatrice, "Right away, I knew I was going to marry the girl wearing the white crane pendant."

She gave it to Harold as a sign of good luck before he shipped out. Not only did the unit coalesce after the event, but Harold and Beatrice became an item and, through their letter writing, fell in love. Shigeo didn't make it. As Harold wrote in a letter to Beatrice, her brother was killed in the Rome-Arno campaign.

"This is my grandfather who raised me," Elaine said as Jordan moved across the room, extending his hand.

"Sir."

"Aloha," the old man said, using the greeting of his origin.

He struggled but rose to a position of attention, took Jordan's hand, shook it with firm conviction, and slumped back down in his chair.

Jordan felt sure, *Yeah, he's an old-timer, but I bet he can still kick some ass if he had to.*

Elaine left the room and returned with Jordan's letter jacket wrapped in her arms. "Here, I wanted to give it back. Do you still ride bikes?"

As he took it, he felt something inside the pocket. It was a small box. Before he could open it, Elaine softly touched his hand.

"Later," she said.

He placed the box in his pocket and gave Elaine back the jacket. "You keep it. I move around too much. I'll lose it."

She searched Jordan's eyes for a moment before taking it back. "Okay, I'm glad it's staying with me. Wearing it makes me remember."

As she turned away, she said, "I have dinner I'm making that can't wait any longer. Sit and talk to my gichan."

Gichan reached for the remote and turned off the game. "You look k`ane to me, so I want to speak man to man. Heard Elaine say you served," the old man said.

"Yes, sir," Jordan answered, trying to remain respectful.

"What?" The old man cupped his hand behind one ear.

"Army," Jordan tried a little louder.

"Rajah, I was in Italy, June of 1944. We lost a lot of boys."

Jordan was about to say Somalia, but instead chose to remain silent.

"Let me talk one story with you. I'm going to talk with you because Elaine said you are ohana. So I can trust you." Gichan went on, "You seen a lot of death. You look like you seen it."

Jordan didn't answer. He didn't need to; the old man knew about death.

Gichan reached for the pack of Camels on the table next to him, lit a cigarette, and took a long drag before exhaling the smoke into the air.

"Gichan, I smell something. Is someone smoking?" came a call from the kitchen.

Gichan looked at the cigarette stuck between his two fingers and smiled. "I don't have much time. I'll be done soon." He paused as a coughing fit took him. "The cigarettes finally caught me."

"I am worried. Elaine looks hamajang. You keep an eye on her after I'm gone."

It wasn't a request, but an order.

"Yes, sir."

Gichan handed Jordan a writing pad and pencil. "Give me a number where I can reach you. Leave it over there by the telephone."

Jordan scratched his name and cellphone number onto the paper and placed it near the old push-button telephone.

He kept one eye on Gichan and one on the lit cigarette dangling between the old soldier's wrinkled fingers. As Gichan spoke, the ash grew longer and longer, not daring to fall off.

"Why not take her to Hawaii to remember small kid times? She's acting all holoholo after the haoles killed her grandma," Gichan said. "They didn't help her much after. Nothing but choke kine problems."

He paused to take a final drag before snuffing the butt out into a full ashtray. "I'm past my prime now. Otherwise, I would take care of business myself. I need your word. Promise you will take care of her, because if anything happens . . . She's all I got. I got your word?"

Jordan got to his feet and went to shake the old veteran's wrinkled hand. The old man stood and saluted. Jordan felt his chest swell with pride. He was honored. The idea that this decorated combat veteran saw something worthwhile in him meant everything. Jordan came to the position of attention and returned his salute.

———————————————————

Elaine hugged Jordan's arm against the evening chill. "You like my Gichan?" she asked as she walked him to his car.

"He's a hero."

The words made Elaine smile. "He liked you. I could tell."

"How do you know?"

"When I introduced you, he said, 'Aloha.' Gichan is old-school Hawaiian and wouldn't say aloha to some random haole he's meeting for the first time. It's how people greet each other but also express love, respect, and gratitude. Tourism stole the word, but to locals, it goes much deeper. He likes you."

"What's a haole?" Before Elaine could answer, Jordan asked, "Is Christian a haole?"

"He's a coconut."

"What?"

"You know, brown on the outside and white on the inside."

"What about you?" Jordan asked.

"I'm a Twinkie," Elaine said. "Yellow on the outside and white on the inside."

"So what's a haole?"

"You."

Chapter Ten

Amber pulled up and parked behind the bar. It was a hot summer day, past noon. Still steaming, she unfriended her boyfriend from her phone. This was the first step after arguing with the asshole, before game-planning how she could exact some revenge on him.

"Threesome. I don't think so! Why are cops such creeps," she said under her breath.

She strolled into the Grand National Bar. The National was the local police bar, tucked away on 12th Street. Down from all the development and around the corner from the new convention center. It might have, at one time, been grand, but it had long since lost its grandeur.

She sat in the back in one of the brown plastic-covered booths near the shuffleboard table. The booth tables were nailed to the floor to prevent their being picked up and catapulted across the room. It was that kind of bar. You had to be careful when you sat down, or you might get poked by the puffer fish lanterns that swam suspended over each booth. It was a sports bar before sports bars were a thing.

The Dax 12-foot shuffleboard table was the centerpiece — so old it didn't cost anything to play. The pinball machines cost a quarter. After the baking sun, the A/C and dim lighting were a welcome relief.

It was that in-between time. The afternoon crowd had finished drinking their lunch and already had gone back to their jobs. There wasn't a single person in the bar, so she thought, beyond the bartender — a young college kid working part-time, wearing his ball cap on backwards, trying to look cool. He didn't look up, focused instead on washing glasses, being careful not to break one over the ice bin.

Amber didn't have a real plan beyond getting pissed-off drunk. She had stopped the habit a long time ago, after dropping out in her junior year of high school to have a baby.

I'm not fat. I'm pleasantly plump. A thought that always returned during breakups — and the reason she drank her vodka with Diet 7 Up.

Looking at her glass before taking a swig, she thought to complain at first, but chose instead to take a white paper napkin and wipe away the proof of how careless College Boy was. *Forget it.* She took a big gulp of the vodka. *Maybe College Boy should focus less on not breaking glasses and more on cleaning the lipstick off them,* she thought.

Halfway into her next cocktail, Amber saw a woman crossing the floor. She approached Amber's booth.

"My name is Avery. Can I buy you a drink?"

The name Avery would work for now, Bellamy decided. Like the U.S. Marine Pathfinders who use branches and leaves to cover their tracks, leave no trace of having been, and wipe their tail to ensure they're not being followed, Avery was her cover.

Amber extended her hand. She shook hands like a man. She had a good, strong grip that came from making a living hanging upside down from a pole. Residual glitter on her cleavage confirmed it.

Not many considerates in this town, Amber thought.

Her jerkoff boyfriend was no different. If he didn't utter the words, he showed it on his face. Amber's hyper-insecurities were highlighted by her green and purple hair and the constant attempts at remaking herself. A lack of self-esteem — one of many reasons why, when the asshole was in the room, Amber took her clothes off in the dark. Even when he wanted to buy her a naughty outfit, she wouldn't go for it.

Maybe her hurt feelings were the reason why she accepted Avery's offer of a drink.

They sat for a long time as Amber went through the list of failed relationships in her life — without apology.

Unfortunately for the bartender, he was born a male. Poor slob had no clue why Amber kept referring to him as a mother-fucker every time he dropped off another round of drinks.

Amber, not bothering to take a breath, droned on about all her problems until she realized Avery wasn't speaking, just taking it all in. "Avery, why don't you stop hogging the conversation," Amber said sarcastically, laughing.

At some point, in the dim light of the bar, Amber formulated her idea to get back at the dumbo. *Revenge-fuck scheme. I'll send dipshit a video of me having some me time with Avery.*

She smirked at her new friend, brushing her hair back from her face. "Screw him," Amber said. "Avery, do you want to get out of this place?"

Amber slid from the booth and followed Avery, who led her out the side door. Not that it mattered — the bartender was in the supply room, too busy restocking shelves to notice them leave.

Outside, Amber kissed Avery on the lips. "Meet up the street at the Corner Liquor Mart," she told Avery. "Park on the side of the building."

Amber stumbled out of the store, pushing the door with her shoulder, careful not to drop the brown paper bag she carried in both hands.

Sliding into the front seat next to Avery, the console prevented Amber from touching her. They sat in Avery's roomier car. The A/C in Amber's sub-compact wasn't working right anyway — another irritant that reminded her of how much of a jerk Cerna was. *He promised to pay to have it fixed.*

They finished off several of the mini's Amber bought from the mart.

Amber, too drunk to drive but now less inhibited, slurred, "You know, I really don't have to depend on anyone. I can take care of myself. I've worked all kinds of jobs all my life."

Avery asked, "What was your favorite position?"

On cue, Amber blurted, "Face down with my ass in the air!"

"I meant your job."

"So did I," Amber laughed. "Who needs a man?" She fumbled through her purse, retrieving a pink sex toy. Doing her best Al Pacino impersonation, Amber said, "Say hello to my little friend!"

Avery, a little nervous, looked around to make sure no eyes were watching.

Amber's tiny condo was close by, so she left her car tucked against the side of the store. Drawn to the rumble from the big engine, she wanted a ride home in Avery's car anyway. It reminded her of the cars her older brother always owned — big block engines, American-made.

The night had started to chill. She didn't have much time to carry out her dirty deed. *Dickhead might change his mind and want to get back with me tonight.*

They drove into Amber's neighborhood. Avery scanned for witnesses while Amber slurred the lyrics from the song playing on the radio.

In that high-density neighborhood, it was always a chore to find parking. Fortunately, Amber's driveway was clear. The nearby homes and apartments were occupied by multiple families. Resources overused, trash bags overflowing out of the dumpster in the apartment complex across the street. Avery backed the Dodge Hellcat into the driveway, leaving room for the garage door.

Amber climbed out and punched the combination to open it. Avery backed in and killed the engine. The quiet was loud. She climbed from the Dodge, grabbing a backpack from the back seat. It momentarily went black when Amber closed the garage door. The ray of light was relieving when Amber opened the door leading into the house.

"Please excuse the clutter," she apologized.

Amber's condo was an allergy sufferer's nightmare. The smell of mold, dusty furniture, and unvacuumed carpet attacked Avery's sinuses. She walked past days of dishes left in the sink. The clutter and food items on the counter, meant for the refrigerator, contributed to the assault of odors.

Carefully stepping around cardboard boxes of Christmas, Easter, and Thanksgiving decorations, dirty clothes, and an assortment of items that would be a junkman's dream, they walked hand in hand to the bedroom.

This isn't clutter — it's a shithole, thought Avery.

While Avery went to the bathroom to find relief, Amber quickly took off her top and bra, then stripped off her jeans and tossed them on the floor. Leaving her underwear on, she threw the blanket aside and got in bed. She kept the lights off — no need for lights. Somewhere in the back of her mind, modesty tried reminding her she was a lady. She reached into her purse like so many nights before, instinctively knowing where it was. She grabbed her little friend and placed it on the bed.

As Avery walked out of the bathroom into the darkened bedroom, Amber peeked through the corner of her eye. "Nice bod," she whispered, feeling extremely fortunate.

She may have concluded otherwise had she looked in the bathroom and inside the backpack. She may have found it curious or even been insulted by Avery's garments meticulously folded in a stack on the counter, neatly covered in a plastic bag.

Seeing the rope and second folded plastic bag, she would have felt outside her comfort zone, having mistaken Avery's intentions. Too kinky for her.

But Amber didn't see because she was distracted by the game she was intent on playing. On your mark! Get ready! Get set! Revenge! Winning at all costs — even if it meant being face down with her ass in the air.

Amber sensed movement behind her and felt Avery's weight sink into the mattress. She felt a hand take her by the waist, never bothering to remove what Amber was still wearing. Neither spoke.

The only sound was of Amber exhaling a soft moan as she felt Avery press up against her. In a rhythm, she opened her eyes for a moment, realizing, *Damn. I forgot to get my cellphone ready to take a video.* But it wasn't close enough for her to reach without having to stop. She thought about it, but she was beyond stopping. Had she been recording, she could have chronicled what was to come next.

Amber enjoyed Avery's increased tempo and pushed back. She felt a hand move from her hips up the middle of her back and pull her hair. Amber was no stranger to hair-pulling as a part of lovemaking — she liked that it added to the experience. Cerna liked pulling her hair. She guessed it was a cop thing.

What she had never experienced before was a scarf around her head. One of Amber's last thoughts was, *Okay, something new.*

At first, Amber felt a swelling pleasure, fueled by the pain, but then came the gradually increasing burning sensation in her neck and shoulders. Not a burning excitement, but a different kind of burn: intense pain. Her agony increased as her head was pulled back, and she felt the tendons and soft tissues in her neck strain. The nerves in her shoulders radiated pain as her vertebrae started to compress. She squeezed her eyes, closing off the sight of her ceiling fan. She tried to force her neck back to an almost normal position. In a vain attempt to stop the pain, Amber said, "You're hurting me! Ass—!"

She was momentarily relieved as the scarf shifted from her head, now around her throat — only to have Avery climb onto her back and wrap her torso in a leg scissor lock. Her eyesight became blurred as the flow of oxygenated blood to her brain was interrupted. She gasped at the strangulation from the scarf. She passed out.

Now unconscious, it was only a matter of time — Amber would be dead soon. Not from a lack of oxygen to the lungs, but from a lack of blood to the brain. Unable to move, life left her body. Finally, when Amber stopped moving, Avery released her grasp.

Avery searched for a moment for signs of life. There were none. She looked around the room and listened for unfamiliar sounds. As she did, something triggered inside her.

It overwhelmed her nature. She couldn't resist the urge to wash the dishes. It was a sign. "Can't stand leaving dishes in the sink," she said. "I need order."

In the end, Avery was glad she had taken the time to tidy up Amber's condo. It was hard enough lugging Amber's body from the bedroom to the garage. The unintended upside of cleaning up was not having to drag Amber around all the crap on the floor.

Kirkland Tow Company came and got Amber's car after it had been abandoned in the liquor store parking lot for about a week. There wasn't much reason for her family or anyone else to be concerned, as she would usually call when she needed money. Kid was with Dad for two weeks. Her rent was paid up.

Chapter Eleven

Elaine prepared dinner on Jordan's final night before returning home. The sashimi, miso soup, and katsu chicken reminded Gichan of the way Beatrice used to make it. Bachan had taught Elaine well.

Gichan got Elaine to show a rare smile when he told her, "Elaine, this meal really broke da mouth." Seeing Elaine smile made for a great night.

"Elaine, when is the last time you seen your girlfriend . . . what's her name?" Gichan said.

"You mean Bellamy? She's around," Elaine said. "Why do you ask?"

"Oh, she just took a liking to the dolls in the hallway. Was asking me about them, that's all."

Jordan, uneasy, shifted in his chair.

"Yeah, where's she been? I haven't seen her in a long time either," Jordan lied.

In reality, he had promised Bellamy he would sneak by to see her on his way home. He needed to thank her anyway for detailing his car after borrowing it the day before. On many nights, he stayed; tonight would be no exception.

Gichan took his cane in hand and shuffled off to bed. Elaine, after tidying up around the house, retired to her bedroom.

Usually, a shower worked just fine, but tonight, Elaine decided it was a good night for a bubble bath and a face mask. She lit candles and turned on the music, a tribute to Bachan. "To the only other man in your life: Perry Como."

Coming out in her bathrobe, with a towel wrapped around her wet hair, bare-footed, she walked down the hallway to say good night to Gichan.

Gichan was quiet.

He already went to sleep, Elaine thought as she stuck her head into Gichan's bedroom. "Goodnight Gi — Gichan?!"

Jordan didn't get the news until the next day, after he'd reached home, when Detective Jake Connely, from Claypond PD, called asking about Elaine's whereabouts. He did not waste time, racing his Hellcat to the house.

Detective Connely, his beer belly held back by a black basket-weaved belt, straining its every fiber, light blue short-sleeved shirt, sweat under the armpits, and a cheap tie, held out a business card. Jordan instinctively took it.

Holding out his fat, sweaty hand, the detective said, "I found your number by his phone."

Jordan obliged the detective and immediately regretted his decision, wiping Connely's sweat onto his pant leg.

"Thanks for coming out. We found the victim in the first bedroom," he told Jordan.

"Gichan?" Jordan asked.

"Is that the old man?" Connely said.

"Yes, that's what Elaine called him."

Elaine's grandfather was found on the floor, a bullet hole through the head from a German Luger he'd kept from the war.

"What the . . . What the hell?!" Jordan blurted out in shock.

"We think he did it to himself, wrapped a towel around the gun to muffle the sound — a suicide," volunteered the detective.

"There's no way!" Jordan's mind raced.

"You mentioned Elaine," Connely said.

"Yeah, where is she?"

"Don't know," Connely answered. "We were hoping you could tell us."

Where was Elaine? He prayed that she was safe.

"I wish I knew," Jordan said to Connely.

"We're trying to locate her. She's next of kin." The detective used a white folded handkerchief to wipe sweat from his forehead. "Let us know if you hear from her."

"Okay, I will," Jordan said, still in shock.

"You might as well go home and get some sleep. I'll call you if I hear or find out anything else," Detective Connely said. "Go on home. The worst is over."

———————————————

Connely's suggestion did nothing to help Jordan that night. It was a night of no sleep — he was busy wondering where Elaine was. The next day, exhausted and sleep-deprived, he sat in a daze, half-awake and half-asleep, in his recliner.

Elaine will be okay, he thought. *She's a survivor.*

But despite Connely's assurance, the worst was not over. The phone rang him back to reality. It was Detective Connely wanting to meet with him at the Tahiti Motel off Beach Blvd. It was about to get really bad.

Jordan found Detective Connely trying not to step on the firefighter's hoses, standing next to the fire engine in front of the charred remains of a burnt-out hotel room.

"It's been a busy couple of days. Remember when I told you it couldn't get any worse? I lied," Detective Connely said. "Think we found your Elaine."

Connely kept using "we" as though he had been there during the time of the fire. "From underneath the door, we saw yellow and red and felt the heat," he went on to explain. "We couldn't go in the room. It was already up in flames. Looks like it's starting to become a murder-suicide to me."

Detective Connely showed professional courtesy, giving Jordan more details than he needed to. He put this hand on Jordan's shoulder. "We tried, but the fire was too hot. We got pushed back by the heat and flames. One of my guys would have burned alive if he didn't get out just before the roof collapsed. Fire guys discovered her on the bed."

All Jordan could mutter was, "How do you know . . ."

"That it's her?" Connely said, jumping in. "Looks like her . . . well, what's left . . . huh, trust me, it's her."

"Positive ID?"

"Look, take my advice. I been doing this a long time. Stop torturing yourself. You can't bring her back," Connely said. "Hotel clerk confirmed Elaine's name is on the room. We'll be in touch if we have anything more for you." The detective handed him a business card.

Jordan reached into his jacket pocket. "You gave me one already."

As he walked away, needing to find a quiet place to sit and cry alone, he thought, *What will Christian think?*

That evening, as forensics put the final touches on the evidence collected from the charred room, the two officers who stood by, maintaining the integrity of the crime scene, stepped into the shadows for an unauthorized smoke break.

Jordan had spent the entire time in his car, parked near the burnt ruins. As darkness came and the moon began to rise, he lay unseen in the backseat of his car, the opened box Elaine had given him on his chest. He fingered the small silver band, watching the moonlight reflect off the tiny amethyst. He brought it to his lips and kissed it. Voices came from the hotel ruins. He wasn't sure, at first, what he heard.

As he lay quietly, one officer exhaled smoke into the air. "Hey, Pasteur, did the lab guys get all the boxes packed?"

"I guess. Now I work for you?"

"Dude, will you stop crying?"

The officers were not aware of Jordan's presence in the backseat of the Dodge. Had they known, it would not have ended well.

Jordan, before today, was not one hundred percent certain about Elaine's story. Not until he heard the officer, taking the last drag off his cigarette and extinguishing it under his boot, say, "Ding dong, the bitch is dead."

"Yeah, snitches get stitches."

Rice and Pasteur exchanged soft laughter, then stood and watched as the forensic van left the area.

There's no way I just heard that. But he did. Elaine was right.

Jordan could feel his concealed weapon pressed against his hip. He touched it over his shirt.

He had every opportunity to make things right. Both officers were distracted, and Jordan had the drop on them.

Easy. Step out from cover. Pop! Pop! Both are dead before they even know what hit them.

It took every ounce of effort not to reach for it and execute both right on the spot. Instead, he waited.

If I do this, I'm just like them, he thought. *No, we're the good guys.*

As he heard their engines rev, he took a slow peek over the dash, just in time to see the two Claypond City PD black-and-whites disappear around the corner. All doubt was now removed.

"Fuckers!"

Chapter Twelve

The two Claypond City Police Officers killed in the explosion were buried after a ceremony conducted at the Graceful Redeemer Church.

They memorialized Officer Jeremy Pasteur and Corporal David Rice, who were then laid to rest.

Reporters asked, but officials would not speculate on any findings in the investigation. Sources closest to the case did say there were persons of interest who needed to be interviewed, but there was no reason to believe at this time that the officers were specifically targeted.

The officers' memorial service, filled with pomp and circumstance, was attended by representative police officers, city officials, and VIPs from throughout the state.

Chief Howell Davis spoke eloquently and eulogized the fallen comrades as good cops.

Misty eyes squinted into the bright sun as the gold Hughes single-rotor helicopters appeared on the horizon.

Always an impressive show, the five choppers flew over, with two peeling off on their own. The others remained in echelon right formation and flew directly over all the mourners. Symbolic of the souls alone on a journey, it tugged at the heart.

The guy with the bagpipes, standing off by himself in a small outcropping of Japanese Black Pines, wore a traditional Highlander outfit — red and black plaid, white spats, and a tall black fur hat with a crop of red running up the side.

When he played "Amazing Grace", even the biggest and the toughest broke down. The tears flowed down their faces as grown men and women in full dress uniforms stood at attention, fingertips gently touching the corner of each temple, hands angled toward the sky in a salute. The white handkerchiefs were a stark contrast against the cadre of dark blue, tan, and green uniforms.

Chapter Thirteen

Chuck built bombs and caused fires. He was good at it. His problem was he liked weed, and his habit caused him to get sloppy.

Chuck agreed to an obligation, and money changed hands accordingly, but his last contracted mission had caused some concern.

Despite providing assurances that the fire would look like an accident, Chuck's carelessness was now a liability.

Smalltown PD is one thing, but had the Feds gotten involved, things would have been much different. Chuck was supposed to make it look like a suicide and arson.

Chuck switched the radio channel. The talk radio guy, Lenny "The Lapper", was going off on a caller.

"You know people take diametrically opposed positions on the issue of police brutality."

Chuck, shaking his head unconsciously, thought back to the time his life turned. Arrested going through New Mexico while still in his soldier's uniform, medals and all. So he had some weed in his pocket.

"Cop could have cut me some slack, being a combat veteran and all," Chuck said, speaking to the radio.

Marcy was happy. She didn't want her baby daddy deploying anymore anyway, but the general discharge made it difficult for him to find a good-paying job.

The Army taught him a skill, and with no legitimate prospects, he went into business on his own. To feed the family, sometimes doing your best is not good enough — sometimes you got to do what it takes.

Chuck, willing to give the radio call-in guest a few seconds more of his time, listened. He promised Marcy he would wait until he got rid of the kids before cranking his favorite "Fuck the Police" CD.

The Lapper shouted, "A good cop gets caught up!"

Chuck muttered, "No such thing as a good cop."

"What, Dad?" came a tiny voice from the back seat.

"Nothin'."

The DJ started on his tirade, "Cops, in the hands of juries that don't know what cops do every day! Yeah, you can decide while sitting on the couch, slurping down a smoothie! Cops make the same decision in seconds."

Chuck flipped the bird at the radio, low enough to make sure the kids didn't see.

"You dance to the music, you got to pay the band, baby! Why do you think San Fran is like it is? No longer illegal to poop on the sidewalk."

Lapper claimed the mean streets of South-Central Los Angeles, but Jared, the sound engineer, knew The Lapper from his college days. They'd been brought up in the streets of San Marino.

"We'll take the next call after a commercial break."

That guy's so full of it, Chuck thought as he pushed one of his wife's CDs into the car stereo. *What an idiot*!

Chuck was not loving life — or driving his own car. He was not used to driving Marcy's Odyssey and didn't like it. An old chick car. Not fast enough to outrun anything. Although Chuck was referential when he described the car, making sure there was no mistaking that, when he said old, he was talking about the car, not Marcy.

The kids screaming in his ear compounded the frustration.

"If I have to tell you all one more time to shut the hell up, you're all gonna get it!"

Now he'd gone and done it, knowing he had just violated rule number whatever of Marcy's "Million Man Rules." He felt a twinge of guilt and shame, but he didn't care at this point. He was pissed.

"I'm going to tell Mom you said hell," threatened Trinity.

He glared into the back seat, giving Conner, Trinity, and Cory the stink-eye through the rear-view mirror. Thank goodness that the package on the front seat, safe if there were no detonators attached, prevented the kids from sitting shotgun.

He was not in the mood to answer a bunch of questions like, "Why does the sun only come out in the day? What's an Adam's apple? Is there such a thing as an Adam's nipple?"

Chuck looked back and saw Conner sitting between his older brother and sister without his seat belt. Chuck yelled at Cory to get his brother's belt on.

"It's broken, remember? You said you were going to fix it," Cory reminded his father as Chuck negotiated the car through the pecan orchards down Sun Beach Blvd toward Dawson Street.

Maybe the yelling at the kids, the radio, thinking about his car repairs, or all of it combined distracted Chuck. He could feel the pressure building inside. He was stressed because he had to be on time, make things right.

Chuck had been an engineer while in the Army. A bomb disposal guy — not EOD, but an Army grade sapper. Having been kicked out of the service against his will, his civilian specialization was mixing hydrogen peroxide and Tang in just the right amounts to blow stuff up.

The package on the front seat of his wife's car needed delivering after dropping off the kids. Chuck was trying to make it right after screwing up the last two times.

"Go ahead and keep fucking up," Avery warned. "We will have to terminate our business relationship."

When confronted, Chuck admitted he had smoked a joint of the good stuff and slept late. In his rush, he had mixed the product while high. His habit was causing him to slip up.

As a result, the first package didn't do exactly what it was supposed to do. Chuck had given assurances that the hotel would be a complete loss. Part of the hotel room was left standing. The second time, no better. Yes, both officers were dead, but Pasteur in a coma for two days wasn't part of the deal.

Chuck became one of the unforgiven when he started feeling froggy and told Avery, "If you don't like it, you can go somewhere else." He unknowingly signed his own death warrant.

As Chuck texted the client that he was thirty minutes out, panic set in as he felt the back end of his car fishtail out of control. The pit maneuver caused Chuck to over-correct, sending the car spinning across the lane, barely missing a fire hydrant, and speed-wobbling into a large pecan tree down an embankment where it came to rest.

Chuck would never have to be bothered anymore by questions raised by his kids or deals that had gone sideways.

As he slumped, semi-conscious, in the driver's seat, he thought he could hear his kids' voices faintly echoing from the inside of a cave.

Viewed through the lens of a concussion, he saw a figure approach without uttering a word or acknowledgment. A gloved hand reached into the car through the shattered window and unlocked the rear door. Connor, Cory, and Trinity were carefully guided away from the wreckage. All held hands as the angel of mercy walked them far enough away from the impending blast area. Chuck felt relief, thinking a rescue person was there to help aid his children.

But the figure walked back up to the car.

"What the hell? Avery?" Chuck whispered.

Avery pulled a BIC disposable from a front pocket and calmly stood by Chuck's shattered window. Chuck, about to utter words of thanks, saw the black leather glove, clutching a lighter, and a closed fist coming toward his face. The punch wasn't heavy but still hurt as it landed.

Avery opened the passenger side door and removed from her pocket an M-80. She lit it and shoved the firecracker between the seat and the package. Chuck heard the door slam shut.

Chuck knew explosives. He bragged that he had made them from urine, ammonia, and C-4. He joked, "Who needs Viagra to get a boner when all you need is some nitroglycerin?" Most of all, he knew what it took to initiate them: a big enough spark.

The base of the tree held the driver's side door locked in place, yet he still scrambled in vain to unbuckle his seatbelt, already knowing it was too late. He reached for the package. Marcy would never forgive him.

When the M-80 detonated, the explosion disintegrated any evidence. The car was completely engulfed in flames. Chuck was dead before the flames incinerated his remains.

The first responders said the wreck was not that bad. Chuck might have gotten away unscathed — that is, if the car hadn't exploded. The kids were turned over to Child Protective Services. Marcy was on her way.

And standing among the shattered remains, busted windows, pieces of taillights, gnarled fenders, and spilled petroleum products were the two officers who were handling the accident scene. Veterans of countless fatalities, the O.G., as they were nicknamed by the younger state troopers, were saddened by the tragedy as always.

The tow truck driver, a grungy-looking sort on his third double in a row, looking like he wasn't supposed to be seen out in the light of day, hooked up the last of the wreckage. As he worked, the two highway patrolmen talked discreetly.

"Screw that! We ate Chinese the other day. I'm burned out on Chinese. Let's go over to the steak place. They do half-price for cops in uniform."

The other said, "How about we go eat waffles? For some reason, I feel like waffles. My mom, when I was little, used to feed us waffles and Tang. You know that orange drink you'd mix with water. Does it smell like Tang around here to you?"

"Yeah, your momma's poontang."

"You're friggin stupid."

They walked away chuckling, crunching pieces of plastic under their black boots as they headed to their patrol cars, amber take-down lights flashing, blocking the road. The tow truck driver, who had finished sweeping up the last of the mess, noted that the tips of some of the pecans were burnt.

Chapter Fourteen

Jordan watched as the news broadcaster talked about the deaths of Officers Pasteur and Rice. The comfort of the gray overstuffed leather chair, in a small measure, helped him relax. He turned on some old-time rock and roll and sipped the 10-year-old Henry McKenna single barrel he'd poured over a round ice cube. He was calm. Call it a revelation, karma, or a coincidence. Nature has a way of making things even in the end.

He had kept his word, though he was perturbed that Pasteur and Rice had not met death at his hands. Accidental or intentional, it didn't matter — it still depletes you.

The news media reported the deaths as an unintended tragedy. A broken gas main. Had they known the truth, it would have caused a storm.

Jordan wasn't sure, but he knew there could only be a few who would toast Pasteur and Rice's deaths, and they were not in the game. Was there someone else playing the game? Who? He had a hunch, knowing that Bellamy had shown a keen interest in meeting Jordan's old Army buddy, Chuck.

Chuck was the only guy that Jordan was aware of who knew explosives and had a chance of carrying this type of incident out. That is, except for Christian. Now Chuck was dead.

If Bellamy was involved somehow, she had to be working from only one emotion: anger. The only question was, to what degree? And how far was she willing to take the game?

Chapter Fifteen

After the memorial service for Pasteur and Rice, their fellow officers stood around, removing their ties and white gloves, discussing tactics. Nothing can be done when it happens like it did. A routine call for service. An open door is how it was dispatched. Nothing could be further from the truth.

"A straight ambush," said the whispers going around the station.

"This was a setup. But who would have the balls to come after the police?" a comment came over the lockers.

"Outlaw motorcycle gang, organized crime — this was a top-shelf hit. It had to be," came a reply.

Sinofsky, the ex-homicide detective, said, "They must not have seen anything that would have hinked them up. How many open-door calls have they seen? Must have thought everything was routine. Just a routine open-door call. How many times do officers respond to open doors?"

Protocol would dictate being careful, but most of the time, it was a big nothing-burger. This time was different.

Officer Pasteur and Corporal Rice didn't stand a chance. They answered the call. The door was ajar. It had happened to all of them before. It was just a part of the job. Eventually, every cop would have to walk through a similar door.

When they made entry into the business, how could they have known that pushing on the open door was the trigger for the mechanism that tripped the blasting cap in the C-4?

"Blew the heck out of the place, killing them instantly. Broken gas main my butt," Womack said. He was a senior officer who had assisted Pasteur and Rice many times. "They were solid officers."

Despite the normal vernacular of the police locker room, Womack wasn't one to use profanity, especially in the presence of ladies — even lady cops. But Womack was hurting and angry, and he lashed out. "This whole fucking . . . fuckers . . . fucked!"

Tough cops got up and walked out, rubbing their eyes. Others just sat in silence, angry.

In stark contrast, the funeral for Gichan and Elaine was a lonely affair. The urn that carried Elaine's remains was placed with Gichan's. A flag draped Gichan's casket. Most of Gichan's war buddies had already gone ahead of him, and the others were too old to travel. They sent nice flowers. The funeral was attended by the mortuary staff and the reverend — all paid to be there.

There should have been two flag-draped caskets, yet there was only one. The employee operating the backhoe was the only one concentrating on Gichan's casket, not wanting to drop it in the hole. No one paid much attention, except for the two figures standing off together under the magnolia tree.

"I'm glad you could make it to say goodbye," Bellamy said, looking at Jordan.

He looked at the ground. She noticed a familiar silver and amethyst ring on a chain around Jordan's neck but didn't ask.

"I told Elaine I was coming back," Jordan said.

"You did your best, just a little too late," Bellamy answered. "Why didn't you tell me that we had something in common?"

"What's that?" asked Jordan.

"What do you think?"

"We both had secrets?"

"Yes, we both have secrets, and we both made promises. Elaine will hold both of us to the promises we made," Bellamy warned. "Better hold up your end."

"Do you think she ever knew about us?"

"No."

Jordan looked up. "What's the plan?"

"Why don't you come over to the house? I'll make us something to eat." Bellamy took Jordan's arm and walked him to his car.

Chapter Sixteen

Bellamy squatted, one knee on the porch, digging through her purse for her house key. Looking at Jordan, she pointed at a potted plumeria. "There's an extra house key under the pot if you ever want to come in when I'm not home."

Jordan walked over to the large plumeria and, without lifting it, canted the pot and took the single key.

As he walked to the front door, Bellamy was mumbling, "Must be here someplace."

As he unlocked the deadbolt, Bellamy said, "Okay, here they are," proudly holding up a wad of keys.

Jordan smiled and replaced the key in its original spot.

"Thanks, Jordan."

"No worries, Bell."

Bellamy went straight for the kitchen, returning with a cold beer in her hand. She handed it to Jordan, who held it without taking a drink.

"Thanks."

She returned to the kitchen and busied herself with dinner.

Jordan sat on the couch. Without thinking, he placed the ice-cold beer on the coffee table. He sat motionless, watching the condensation form on the side of the full beer. He watched the drops, too heavy, cascade down the bottle, pooling at the base. He started to notice a small puddle forming and suddenly remembered Bellamy's insistence on using coasters. He picked the beer up as condensation dripped onto the table, making things worse. Taking the top coaster from the stack on the table, he set the bottle on it. Looking in the direction of the kitchen, he wiped the water away with his bare hand.

Looking around the room, he spied a box of tissues, then got up and went to retrieve some to clean up the mess.

As Jordan was wiping the residual water from the table, an image suddenly fixed itself in his mind. He saw the kokeshi doll standing next to the box of tissues. Where had he seen it before? Of course! The doll resembled the one he'd seen in Gichan's hallway when he'd been there visiting with the old war hero. As he examined it more closely, he realized it didn't just resemble the one in Gichan's house — it was the one. It was the one-of-a-kind Katase Kaihei Oboroyo. He was sure of it.

Bellamy prepared a nice dinner — chicken fried steak with brown gravy, mashed potatoes, mixed vegetables. Simple, but tastefully done. She offered apple pie, but Jordan declined. She was a cordial host, and they drank Chardonnay during dinner.

Jordan helped clear the dishes and waited for the right time. The dishwasher was running the plates, silverware, and cutlery through the rinse cycle before he finally brought it up.

They sat at the dinner table sipping whisky, an empty dessert plate in front of Bellamy. Jordan, making small talk, asked Bellamy, "How do you eat apple pie and drink whiskey?"

"I use a fork," she said, smiling.

In the dim light, Jordan said, "I like your Asian decorations. I noticed the doll. My mother had a couple."

"I like wooden dolls," Bellamy said.

It was obvious by Bellamy's response that she did not know the significance of the piece Jordan was talking about.

"Where did you get that one?" He pointed toward the kokeshi doll. "My mother would love one like that."

Bellamy grew uneasy and said, "Elaine gave it to me for my birthday . . . two years ago." She held out uncertain hope that Jordan would buy the story.

Not wanting to draw more suspicion, Jordan stood up and said, "Before calling it a night, how about a pour of whiskey?"

While Bellamy showered, Jordan lay in bed, mentally notating the day's events before finally dozing off — only to be awakened in the middle of the night by a strange dream. He'd seen the guy walking down a long, darkened corridor, fading further into the darkness. He awoke before having to shoot the Cuban again.

Upon Jordan's return from deployment, Hargrove asked him, "How many times have you had to kill those two guys?"

At first, he didn't understand — that is, until the dreams started coming. Then he knew what Hargrove had been trying to say. Many who have experienced taking a life have to kill their adversary over and over a million times in their dreams. Some reported waking up with the enemy standing at the foot of their beds. Jordan was lucky his dreams never got that far.

He stood over the toilet, relieving himself, taking care not to miss. After all, there were no other men in this house, and he would be blamed for sure. Not using a coaster is a misdemeanor — peeing on the floor or forgetting to put the lid down, a felony offense.

As he tried to think back to sitting and talking with Bellamy, Jordan thought, *Damn, I must have been tired after the cocktail. I don't remember shit. I feel drugged.* He started to stumble back to the bedroom, but stopped when he saw a dim light coming from the living room. He made his way slowly down the hallway to find Bellamy sitting on the couch in her bathrobe.

"You still up?" he mumbled.

"Couldn't sleep," she said. "Go back to bed. I'll be in there soon."

He shuffled back to the bedroom and collapsed in the bed, falling asleep almost immediately.

A few minutes later, Bellamy got up and pressed her ear to the bedroom door, listening for his breathing. Satisfied that he was sound asleep, she shrugged off the concealing robe, put her shoes on, and quietly made her way out the front door.

The next morning, Jordan woke up feeling a bit groggy. He blamed it on the alcohol and carbs. He quickly and quietly got dressed, trying not to disturb Bellamy, who was still asleep.

His car was parked in front of her house. He had parked it in the driveway last night. *She must have moved it.* Not thinking anything of it, he climbed in and cranked the ignition.

The SRT fired up with a low rumble. The seat warmers were nice against the chill of the morning. The infotainment system kicked in with *Carlos Santana and Buddy Miles! Live!* Jordan, nodding his head to the beat, threw it into drive and pressed the pedal. As the car rolled forward, Jordan instinctively looked down at the dash. *I thought I bought gas yesterday. Dude, this thing sucks gas,* he thought.

Chapter Seventeen

Jordan continued to spend the next few months hanging with Bellamy on his days off. She seemed to enjoy his company — his suspicions growing, Jordan tolerated hers. He was willing to sacrifice if it meant he could get to the bottom of what was going on, even if it meant sharing Bellamy's bed.

As he walked out of the gym to his car, checking his messages, his phone rang. It was Reggie Smith, who everyone knew as Smitty.

Smitty and Jordan knew each other from their Army days together. They bragged about their wild times when they could kill off a bottle of scotch with no ill effects the next day. They chuckled about overseas bar girls who picked up stacks of coins with their genitalia and dropped them one by one into servicemen's beer glasses. They saluted the comrades who were no longer with them.

Smitty told Jordan, "This is unofficial."

A rumor was circulating that there had been an attempt on another Claypond cop.

"How do you know?"

"It's out on the streets," Smitty said. "He must have pissed off the wrong person and gotten targeted. Has to be. It looked too much like another hit."

After agreeing to meet for drinks, Jordan hung up the phone. He stood in the parking lot for some time, thinking about what Smitty had just told him. Jordan held out hope that it wasn't who he thought it might be.

"Hey, Christian, you got time to talk?"

"Of course, a few minutes anyway. What's up?" Christian asked.

"Are you allowed to say where you are right now?"

"Yeah, I'm about 6,500 miles from California. Across the Tasman Sea. You want to say hi to Michelle?" Christian, on speaker phone, pointed his phone at Wang.

Wang, in the middle of inventorying medical supplies, looked up.

"Michelle, say hi to Jordan."

"Hi, baby," she said, and went back to her task.

Christian turned off the speaker and asked, "Is everything cool? You're acting more weird than usual."

"Just checking on you, making sure you're staying out of trouble. I haven't heard about any coups or uprisings in a while, and I figured you and your peeps must be getting bored."

While listening to his friend, Christian noticed Donovan digging in a wood pile, looking for something. He watched as Donavan found several Huhu beetle grubs, popped one into his mouth, and began chewing.

He offered one to Christian. "Lunch?"

"You know we do what we gotta do to keep busy. Some of us are better at it than others," Christian said, still sensing something wasn't quite right with Jordan. "You sure you're good?"

"Nah, I'm cool."

"How's Elaine?"

Jordan's heart sank. "It's not good, Christian. She ran into a shitstorm, bro."

"Bad?"

"As bad as it gets . . . dead."

"What? What happened!?" said Christian.

Jordan gave Christian a full account.

"Bro, I'm so sorry. Let me know if I can do anything."

Jordan hung up. On the one hand, relieved, in a sense, having gotten things off his chest. But he still felt lost and isolated even after having spoken to Christian about all the events. He thought it might help, but it did little to alleviate the concern he still had.

At first, Cerna thought the alcohol was making him feel overly paranoid. He'd tried to reach her several times but still hadn't heard anything from Amber. "So, bitch just took off and didn't say squat. After all I did for her."

Cerna's eyes turned to the leftover beer from the night before that sat on the kitchen counter. He finished it. "At least the bitch cleaned up her house before she split."

Scouring his memory, he tried to recall any potential catalysts for his string of bad luck — strange vehicles, people, Amber cutting out.

The question that occupied his mind was the engine he'd heard. Was it the same one near his house days before?

Cerna was an aficionado of classic cars. He grew up around cars, helping his dad and uncles rebuild motors in the backyard. He knew the

396 big block engines found in most Chevy El Caminos, Chevelles, and Camaros and the 3.6L V6 24-valve engine in the Dodge Hellcat by their sounds. The sound he'd heard was definitely a Mopar.

This was not a pro who attacked him. Too many mistakes. First mistake was in the logistics of the mission. There was a certain sense of amateurism to the attempt.

The shooter should have formulated a plan to take out Cerna without leaving any clues. Perhaps the assassin surmised that it wouldn't have made any difference after Cerna was already dead. Their hatred had to be so great that the killer needed to make a point. Cerna was determined to learn who tried to end him and why. This was personal.

Mr. Teri's was a local hole-in-the-wall bar located underneath the I-5 freeway. The area conjured up the stereotypical images found in people's imagination and made them into reality. The district consistently ranked as one of the worst and was considered the infected wart on the broken toe of the city.

The rough part in desperate need of revitalization — but a necessary evil. Where else would the dregs hang out?

It was past closing time, and a small contingent of ginnygogs milled around Mr. Teri's parking lot, saying their goodbyes.

Cerna eventually came pouring out of the bar, his breathing labored. He paused to lean against his Buick to take a quick leak. Using one arm for support, he concentrated on not pissing on his Cole Caiman boots.

He squinted to adjust his eyes to the darkness. A dark shadowy figure approached. It inched closer with Cerna's every exhale. The shooter held the nine-millimeter close enough so only Cerna could hear.

"Cerna," a voice whispered.

Three 158-grain slugs pounded him in the back, just missing his head. The concussion blew Cerna around. He got spun off his feet, landing on the ground, his body half under his car. The shooter, their rage against Cerna satisfied, now took their anger out on the car. But even firing several rounds through the passenger door and window of the '85 Buick Regal wasn't enough. Cerna, semiconscious, felt the parting shot — a kick in the balls.

In that neighborhood, the familiar sound of gunfire was like a call to the wild. People knew not to stick around. Too many with outstanding warrants or at risk of being reported by probation or parole officers itching to send them back to jail.

The noise brought the few law-abiding residents alive. Dogs barked, setting off the chain-reaction howls of other dogs down the street. Porch lights turned on, and people watched through bedroom curtains. It wasn't that dark, yet no one saw a thing. Anyone who did knew better than to open their mouth.

A security guard said she saw a Phantom Black Tri-Coat Pearl Dodge Challenger with blacked-out windows leaving the area. She was certain of it because she had dated a guy with the same car for a while. She broke up with him because he was more in love with his car than with her. Only difference was the color.

Chapter Eighteen

Looking in the mirror, Cerna winced at the sight of deep purple bruising on his back. Bad, but could have been much worse had one of those rounds pierced his armor. He stared, trying to figure out why the owner of the Dodge was after him. It wasn't a professional hit, so what was it? Revenge? An attempt to get rid of competition? What? Squeezing businesses for protection money made so many enemies.

He crossed himself and thanked his patron saint for the Kevlar he always wore, a habit from when he used to believe in God. Bulky, hot as hell, and cumbersome in the summer — but now more than worth the hassle. Cerna wore it because he was not one of those jump-off-a-bridge kind of guys — more like a snipe-from-a-tower type.

It would take some time to recover from his injuries, but in the meantime, there was work to do. Cerna would use his recovery to start working the streets to find out what was up. Who the hell was it who wanted him dead this time? Because of the darkened windows, nobody saw the driver. Unfortunate.

Cerna knew he might only get one chance. *I need to think this shit through. First thing, run the information on the car through the system. Find out who owns it.*

Cerna sat in his patrol car, wincing and still sore. He had only been able to use the flu as an excuse for a few days. He keyed in his user ID and password to begin accessing the local, state, and federal systems through the CLETS on the MDT.

Using the system for personal gain was unauthorized, but Cerna wasn't worried. He was running so many vehicles every day to determine if they were stolen or had expired registration tags. If the DOJ checked him, which they did from time to time, this check would go unnoticed. As the computer fired up, he toggled to the Department of Motor Vehicles database.

Cerna's eyes shifted back and forth, reading the information on the computer screen. He typed in the vehicle description, make, model, and approximate year and got a hit on six matches. He wrote down license plate information on a steno pad and cross-checked against them.

Cerna wasn't sure, initially, what he was looking for, but he'd know it when he saw it. He accessed the vehicle registration database. Of the six vehicle plates, one was salvaged, which meant it had been totaled in an accident.

Cerna read that the second had a citation attached to it for speeding, issued on the day he'd been shot. But it was in Richmond, a suburb of Oakland, over 300 miles away. As he scanned through the information, one jumped out at him. The custom plate read "Gatormn."

It was the only "confidential" registration, which could only mean the owner was in law enforcement or a firefighter. The confidential plate came back to Baldwin City PD.

———————————————

It took Cerna two days of surveillance, watching as the Baldwin cops went off duty, leaving the station.

He heard it first before he saw it. Jordan's dark green Dodge Hellcat pulled through the automatic gate and onto the street. Security guard was half right. SRT Hellcat — but not black. Cerna tailed Jordan to Ustaza, taking care to stay back.

They passed a park with a swimming pool and some basketball hoops, then Jordan parked in front of a mid-century modern home, located down the street from a church.

Nice neighborhood, Cerna thought. *Good place to raise kids*. He noticed the house was well kept, with one side screened off by trees.

While following the Dodge into town, Cerna had seen supermarkets and a hospital. *There ain't no mortuary,* Cerna thought as he slouched down in the front seat of the Corolla and watched Jordan walk toward the house. *And he's gonna need a morgue.*

Jordan, carrying his freshly laundered police uniform in clear plastic slung over one shoulder, knocked on the door. When the front door opened, Cerna caught a first glimpse of Bellamy, who greeted Jordan and let him in.

Staring at Bellamy, Cerna unconsciously adjusted himself. "I got you, fucker."

Cerna's career choice was never about saving the world. It was about being a member of the biggest gang in the country. Not like Rice and the others, who started as idealistic good cops. Something changed in them. Not all at once, but the gradual stress, anger, and frustration blurred the lines between good and bad. Cerna just helped to nudge them over the edge.

Cerna groomed Rice, and Rice groomed Pasteur. That's how it worked. The culture was created as they witnessed their friends getting fired, humiliated, and murdered. It seemed to give some in the profession a reason. No excuses, just justification.

The final straw, the tipping point, was the protests that began to mount against cops. The attention that should have fallen on unscrupulous individuals fell on their beloved profession instead.

"Society doesn't give a fuck about us; we don't give a fuck about them." Cerna fed the fire. "You think all cops are dirty? Okay, we'll show you what dirty really looks like."

But Cerna was a different breed. He should never have made it past the application process. Specifically, the psych test. He had been a cop most of his adult life and did not hide behind the badge.

Not like this piece of crap, he thought as he slowly drove past Bellamy's house.

Cerna, a crooked cop, knew and accepted what he was. Life and all its unfairness pushed him to be part of a gang long ago. Growing up, he had been taught street ethics, and to certain people, he didn't lie. He made no bones about it. He'd tell the truth most of the time. He accepted his reality.

If asked what gang he represented, Cerna never backed down. "Before I became a cop or after?"

Although he had never been jumped in, his older brother Mike had and claimed Varrio Viejo gang membership. Cerna's first few PD application process disqualifications were because of Mike, who had spent time in Deuel Vocational Institution, Palm Hall, Chino Men's, and San Bernardino County Jail.

Cerna, ever loyal to his family, never complained, but his family knew the hardships he faced, having to apply to forty police departments before getting picked up. Cerna was never a full-fledged gangster, but his family's history and affiliations certainly affected his getting hired.

Cerna's luck changed one morning in South Bakersfield, on El Alisal Street, near White Lane and Hughes. A double-edged sword, Cerna's employment prospects got better after his brother Mike got shot.

Mike, a hardcore gang member who never denied his affiliation, chose instead to face the consequences.

When a red Chevy Camaro pulled beside him as he walked along a dusty, trash-strewn street, a voice called out, "Where you from, homs?"

Mike fully recognized the intent behind the three words. "Where you from?" could mean "You might die."

Knowing he was caught in the wrong place at the wrong time, Mike still refused to deny his reality. He only needed to utter the words, "I don't gang bang," to save his own life. Instead, Mike did something that he knew would result in serious repercussions.

He stopped and turned, scowling, faced his assailants, and like an orchestra director facing the musicians, held his hands in the air.

With both hands, Mike flashed his gang's sign, pointed at his crotch, and thrust his pelvis in the face of the passenger in the car. To add to the disrespect, Mike yelled, "Que te den por culo!" Something to the effect of, "Shove it up your ass."

Bullets ripped into him. His instinct was to run, so he did — as fast as only a dead man could. Bullets chased him down the street to where he fell. The Camaro stopped, and the passenger exited the vehicle, calmly walked up, and put a round into Mike's head.

The driver yelled, "Let's go!" and the Camaro drove away.

Even after becoming a cop, just like Mike, Cerna never uttered the words, "I don't gang bang!"

Cerna was born in East Bakersfield, close to downtown, near Baker and Sumner Street. His high school was famous for several notables — Rudolph Carmona, a co-founder of the La Piasa Organized Crime Syndicate, the Beltran brothers, Louie and Robert, who were a musician and an actor, and J.R. Sakuragi, who came before Lin-sanity.

"What's the difference between gangs and cops?" Cerna would ask. "Gangs run around at night in packs and carry guns. So do we. Gangs beat people up and kill people. So do cops. We have our own language, uniforms, and code of ethics. So do gangs. What's the difference? Besides, life made me this way," he repeated often.

He made little effort to hide what he was. He wore the scars proudly. He wasn't about to hide in the dark. *Not like the coward who tried to do a hit on me,* he thought.

Cerna sat on a bar stool in La Habana, drinking from a glass of Michelada. He pushed his glass to the edge of the drip tray. "Hey, cabrón, I fucking told you, heavy on the tequila, light on the beer."

The bartender, a 6'5" giant with a full beard and suspenders, without saying a word, took the glass back to add a double shot of Milagro. He set the newly strengthened drink on a napkin in front of Cerna. "Pendejo. Cerna, you know I can cut you off," he warned.

"I'll tow your car, give you a ticket, and then kick your ass," Cerna said, somewhat slurred.

"In your fucking wildest dreams, shithead. Quit being an asshole." The bartender snatched the $10 tip Cerna tossed onto the bar.

The alcohol helped to numb the hurt a bit, but not enough to dissuade Cerna from carrying out his new plan.

Rewinding the idea back through his head — go to the house, kill the chick, and make it look like Jordan did it. Lovers' quarrel. A domestic violence thing. *Got a better idea. I will fuck his life up for being the piece of shit he is. It worked before; it'll work again.*

Jordan would be made to live, fighting every day. He didn't deserve to die a hero, with all the pomp and circumstance. No way was anyone going to cry and memorialize his death.

They are going to erase him from their memories after I finish with him, Cerna thought.

Jordan would spend time in prison for killing his girlfriend — with the same guys he threw in jail. Hopefully, he'd be sitting in PC with all the baby rapists and snitches.

When Jordan was completely burned out and exhausted, Cerna, using one of Mike's old prison connections, would pay good money to have him on his knees, begging for his life. One day, someone would come around and stab the shit out of him.

Would have done the same to Elaine, had the bitch not taken the easy way out and killed herself, he thought. *Lucky for her that Rice and Pasteur were there when we had her on the floor. If it was up to me, I would have made her feel what it was like to be with a real man.*

Cerna would now be the hunter, with Jordan, unknowingly, the hunted.

"Give me a shot of tequila, and not that cheap shit."

Chapter Nineteen

Getting into the house was easy. Bellamy had done a lot of work remodeling the place, but the windows were still old-school and easy to pry open.

Cerna had seen homes like this before but never lived in one. The home had been well cared for and was decorated with a womanly touch. Actual paintings hung from the walls, not those fluorescent naked women on a black velvet background.

The house was older, but Bellamy had decorated it to look more modern. It felt warm and secure — blues and browns, wood and seascapes, an affinity for whales. The magnet on the Bosch refrigerator read, "The more I learn about men, the more I love cats."

Cerna couldn't place the smell at first, but he picked out the scent of dried flowers. It was lavender, a thick aromatic odor. He liked it. He looked at the little wooden kokeshi doll with the round head and curly hair.

Looks oriental. The home had a good feel to it, and Cerna thought, *This smells of normal. Why do shitbags get to be happy?*

For a moment, permitting the distraction, he recalled Donna, the former University of Dayton cheerleader, an ex-old lady turned stripper. The faces she made and the smell of fruit as she threw up from the shots of Bird Dog Black Cherry whiskey or whatever she'd drank too much of. Cerna remembered the times, puke smell, passed out drunk.

And I still did her. He smirked to himself. *Why do I always attract the bimbos? The screwed-up chicks with a carload of baggage, like that train-wreck Amber. What an insecure loser,* he thought.

Another guy would have just left her there. Instead, Cerna was always there to shove ice down the front of her shirt to try and bring her around when she almost OD'd.

Cerna was like that, loyal to people who were loyal back to him. He didn't believe in leaving his partners behind.

He entered the bedroom and saw the canopied bed, a light shade of brown with a light green thick silk comforter. He saw a beige dresser with perfume bottles and a small plate with assorted earrings and silver chains. The nightstands matched the dresser.

On the back of the door hung a thick all-white cotton bathrobe. *This girl keeps her place nice.*

The bedroom was decorated with light green accents. Had he known Bellamy, he would have known her habit of changing her bedroom decor as the seasons changed. Green for fall, blue for winter, and brown for summer.

He touched the cool softness, and he had to test out the bed. As he lay there in the scented quiet, he closed his eyes and tried to imagine what life would be like with her. The blanket on which he rested was nothing like his own.

Cerna, attracted to the vintage Pennsylvania House furniture, stared into the mirror on the dresser. He read her name scrawled on a thank you card: Bellamy.

He wanted to know more about Bellamy, whose inner world he had invaded. Not so much the value of her belongings but more about what kind of things this Bellamy owned.

This girl whose bedroom curtains matched the bed covers. He didn't know her, but felt something inside. He wondered what the connection between her and Jordan was. He felt slight remorse that she had to become a casualty of war.

Nothing like the females he was used to. Most were lucky to have plain sheets covering the sweat- and urine-stained mattresses.

He wanted to learn how she dressed, the type of clothing she wore, what she smelled like. He looked in a dresser and found the drawer that held her undergarments. Bellamy liked the sportier look.

The French cut bikini panties with the matching T-shirt tops that were cut halfway up the midsection. Blue, pink, grey, black — the kind that expose a flat, tight stomach. All meticulously lined up, orderly, all with the exact same folds.

Cerna found six matching pairs, along with a variety of lacy panties and bras. He fingered the garments. They smelled clean and scented. He didn't know why, but he careful to replace each item exactly where he'd found it — except one.

He closed the dresser drawer, reminding himself to tell his next old lady to put bars of soap in the dresser to scent her clothing too. *Why bother? They barely use soap to take showers,* he thought to himself.

In his hour of examining Bellamy's home, he'd learned quite a lot about how the other side lived and how real ladies carried themselves. He found himself becoming more enamored with what he was finding out about Bellamy.

He tried to imagine him and Bellamy living a normal life together in this home. It was just a fleeting thought. He looked further into the back of Bellamy's closet, pushing aside the winter coats.

"Lots of shoes, typical," he said to himself. "Why do the losers get the nice ones?"

Cerna, distracted, hadn't been watching the clock. He suddenly realized he had already spent too much time in the house. He had become so engrossed with looking through Bellamy's personal belongings that he never even noticed her next-door neighbor, Mrs. Hanratty.

Every night between her shows, Mrs. Hanratty took her trash out and gave her wiener dog, BoBo, a chance to do his business.

She spied Cerna through Bellamy's bedroom window, which was adjacent to her own back stoop. Neighbors had always complained that the old bag spent too much time on her porch with her nose in other people's business, listening and watching all the time. Bellamy thought the innuendoes comical.

Mrs. Hanratty did a double-take at first, thinking it was only Bellamy or Jordan walking through the house. But as she raised her flabby arm to acknowledge them, she realized that was not the case.

She ducked behind the porch railing as quickly as a seventy-year-old woman could and peered out between the posts, her hand instinctively covering her mouth. Her eyes locked on him as he moved from the bedroom to where she knew the living room to be. She had to step down off her porch to get a closer look at Cerna as he passed into the kitchen. He was holding something pink in his hand. Mrs. Hanratty jerked her head back and forth, squinting to see if the intruder had company. The only movement was BoBo, his leg hiked, doing his business on the azaleas.

She saw him raise the fabric to his face, as if to wipe something from his mouth, then place the pink cloth into his right-hand jacket pocket.

Mrs. Hanratty was a nosy neighbor, to whom Bellamy showed a courteous tolerance. Sometimes she treated Bellamy too much like a young kid, always checking up on her.

Mrs. Hanratty watched Cerna, not recognizing him. She didn't know the pink fabric she'd seen Cerna sniff was a stolen souvenir from Bellamy's dresser. The perfumed clothing was intoxicating, and even more so to a guy used to dirtbags and drunks he'd pick up. He'd never been with what he considered a real nice lady.

Cerna thought he saw, from the corner of his eye, something flash outside, and he suddenly became concerned. He dreaded the time wasted, not spent on reconnaissance. He had spent far too much time getting to know Bellamy intimately. It was a mistake, and he still had to leave the note before he could get out of there. Through Cerna, Bellamy would find out Jordan was a cop killer — and why Jordan was trying to kill her.

Cerna went into the kitchen and found the notepad kept near the telephone. He took a pen from the drawer, then began to contemplate the words he needed for Bellamy.

Cerna still had not worked out the connection between Jordan and Elaine. If he had, he might have connected the dots between Elaine and Bellamy.

He wrote, "Your boyfriend is not who you think he is. He is a cop killer. You need to notify the authorities."

Cerna knew that any good homicide investigator worth his salt would look through Bellamy's daily planner. He hid the note in the planner and left it on the kitchen counter.

Chapter Twenty

Bellamy, having finished her shift, was headed home. She pushed her card into the card reader, the arm lifted, and she drove out of the police station's back lot.

Her phone rang, and she pulled over to answer it. The phone call was the perfect alibi to move forward with her plan. This was her opportunity to tie up all the loose ends. As she briefed him, Jordan heard in the background someone checking their police siren before driving off to start their shift.

"I just got off the phone with Mrs. Hanratty next door. Said there's somebody skulking around my house."

Jordan said, "I'm off duty. Did you call the police?"

"What the fuck, Jordan? We are the police!" Bellamy said, almost shouting into the phone. "If you don't want to do this for me, have some balls and do it for Elaine," Bellamy scolded. "I'll meet you there." She hung up before Jordan could confirm help was on the way.

Jordan parked his car three houses down, in the shadows, got out, and started walking toward Bellamy's house. He knew this street, having spent many days and nights there. He didn't like the tall trees because of what they did to his paint.

At first, seeing nothing unusual from the front room window, he snuck around to the backyard. From his new vantage point, he saw a figure who stood with his back facing the kitchen window. The same window Jordan stared through.

Jordan thought Bellamy was coming with additional officers, but Bellamy had other plans. No help was coming.

Jordan went to the front and found the key on the patio, under the flowerpot. He was relieved that Bellamy hadn't listened to him and placed a stick in the tracks of the sliding glass door. Jordan unlocked the door slowly, slid it open, and gun drawn, quietly entered the house.

Bellamy also knew her neighborhood well and parked one block south of her own street. The space was tight, but she crawled through a hole in the hedges, disregarding the loose twigs that scraped her face. She crouched in the shadows, invisible to anyone looking out from inside of the house.

She didn't have time to wait. It was important to get close to the action. She didn't want to make any noise for fear of compromising her position to whoever else might be on watch in the yard.

Bellamy hurried to the kitchen window, looked inside, and tried to gauge what was going on. She saw Cerna, wearing a military-style jacket, standing face-to-face with Jordan.

Cerna's arms were down by his sides. Jordan had a gun pointed at him. He seemed to have things under control.

Bellamy couldn't make out what was being said between the two adversaries. She only heard muffled words through the closed window. Cerna raised his hands above his waist, as though he was raising his hands in the air.

She dropped down out of sight to move toward the rear door. But before Bellamy could place her hand on the doorknob, her body instinctively jolted at the thunderous recoil of a 45-long. She heard two rounds, distinctly.

She quickly peeked through the door, at the same time hiding her service weapon under her jacket, then rushed into the kitchen to provide aid.

Jordan lay there, his breathing labored. With each breath he took, blood gurgled up through his throat as air escaped out of the wound created by the silvertip hollow points that had torn into his body. Cerna stood a short distance away, a two-inch 357 Smith and Wesson in one hand and a badge in the other.

He turned toward the sound of Bellamy entering, holding up his badge. "Police officer! Don't be alarmed." He looked at Bellamy. "He's the cop killer."

Chapter Twenty-One

Bellamy, on instinct, opened the kitchen drawer and pulled out a roll of plastic wrap. She didn't bother trying to tear off a neat piece, throwing the roller end to the ground while holding the loose end of the wrapping. With one hand, she placed the wrap over the wound. She tried in vain to stop the air escaping through the bubbling holes. He breathed a few more short breaths, opened his eyes, and tried to speak.

Jordan reached into his pocket and retrieved the worry stone Christian had given him back in Haiti. No longer having the strength to hold it, the stone dropped to the floor. Bellamy took it and placed it in her pocket.

He died, and his accusations died with him, unspoken. She saw Cerna had picked up Jordan's handgun and was on the phone, seemingly calling 911. Bellamy was already one step ahead, calculating that he was only pretending to make a call.

Now to blame Jordan for the murder of his girlfriend, Cerna thought.

While Bellamy tended to Jordan, her back turned to Cerna, he took a steak knife from the drawer Bellamy had left open, putting it in his pocket.

Part two has to happen in the living room to make it look real, he thought.

Bellamy looked back across the room at Cerna. He looked up and met Bellamy's eyes. "Help is on the way," he lied.

As Cerna clipped his badge to his belt and holstered his pistol, he said, "I came here to interview this guy. He's a suspected cop killer."

She stared at Cerna while he continued to talk. Cerna, unaware that Bellamy was ahead of the game, assumed she could empathize with killing a cop killer.

"I'll need to keep the gun as evidence," he said. "Why don't we go into the living room until help arrives? That way, we don't contaminate the crime scene."

He tried to play it official. He felt confident that Bellamy was unaware of his plan to use her as the sacrificial lamb.

Bellamy stood and walked down the hallway to the living room. "All dirtbags should have their tickets punched," she finally said.

Cerna took a breath. "Yeah, no loss. He was dirty."

Bellamy entered the living room, standing in the middle of the floor. Cerna walked to the window and peered into the darkness at a quiet street. Satisfied, he reached into his pocket and pulled out the knife. When he turned around, he was face to face with Bellamy — Cerna with a knife, Bellamy with her service semi-automatic.

"You know this is the end of the shit show. All that was violent and evil comes to an end here."

Not understanding her meaning, Cerna said, "Yeah, it's finally over. Give me the gun." He reached out to take the weapon from Bellamy.

"No you don't," Bellamy said. "I wanted to tell you thanks for your sacrifice. Your old lady, I mean. She made the ultimate sacrifice for the good of the whole. What was her name? Amber?"

Cerna's face told the story of realization and miscalculation.

But Bellamy wanted Cerna to hear it all from her. "You are why she burned in the fire," she said. "Don't fret. If it even matters, she was already dead when I put her on the bed. I was sure that you guys would half-ass the homicide scene. Your friends never noticed it was Amber, not Elaine, burned up on the bed. And the beauty of it all is that Elaine doesn't even know I did it."

Cerna tried to orient his mind around what she was saying. "What the fuck are you talking about? Elaine doesn't know?"

"Yep, you got rid of the threat to my happiness. Thank you. And now I'll get rid of the threat to Elaine's," Bellamy said.

She felt her disgust and anger toward Cerna grow. The realization that Elaine had been right all along. *Stay focused,* she thought. *Complete the mission.*

Bellamy wanted Cerna to feel alone in the world after the death of his girlfriend. But she saw nothing to indicate Cerna felt remorse, even after starting to understand that Amber was dead because of him.

"You know, Elaine was right," she said. "They get no sympathy, those who invaded my . . . our lives."

Then she saw her underwear partially hanging from Cerna's pocket. "You rotten son of a bitch! That vest you're wearing won't help you this time!" She pressed the trigger and fired.

Cerna lurched backward, tumbled, and fell on top of the basket holding all the remotes.

"Dammit! Now I'm going to have to get a new basket," Bellamy said as she watched Cerna, looking for life in his body.

Bellamy pushed the button on her cellphone and took a deep breath. "Officer needs assistance. Shots fired!"

She carefully retrieved her lingerie from the dead man's pocket and left the knife on the floor.

This is going to work out better than I expected, she thought as she heard a siren off in the distance approaching. Deep inside, she felt respite, knowing that in all the confusion, she was still able to remind herself to remain calm.

Bellamy began looking around. She needed to be clear of mind and make sure nothing was left undone before help arrived.

She was content that things would work out. She had been in tough situations before and could handle anything. Besides, she only had to report exactly what she saw and heard, exactly the way it happened. Bellamy smiled.

She examined Cerna's lifeless body. Going back into the kitchen, she looked at Jordan and thought death was so inelegant. Not like those Hollywood movie starlets who always died so beautifully on the big screen.

In Cerna, Bellamy saw evil. He had a look of betrayal. Cops don't kill other cops. In Jordan's face, there was just a blank look.

She felt anger toward Jordan. His death had become necessary. Elaine was starting to fall back in love with him. Bellamy couldn't keep the lie going about Elaine any longer. She could see it in the way Elaine smiled when he was around.

It's your fault, Elaine. Why don't you smile like that for me? I'm not a total monster. I felt something for Jordan. That was real, and it counts for something, right? I wouldn't have had sex if I hadn't been attracted in some small measure, Bellamy lied to herself to rationalize her actions.

"Elaine, you were bait. You should have stayed in your place," Bellamy said out loud. "Cerna and you both tried to steal from me. Get what you get."

Mrs. Hanratty was waiting. She'd been waiting the entire time since she'd seen Cerna prowling around Bellamy's house and called her. She'd shut off her T.V. and lights and was looking out through a crack in her closed curtains. She saw Jordan arrive and recognized him. She saw him enter through the sliding glass door. She saw Bellamy going around to the front and heard the two gunshots that sent her screaming and sprawling to the floor for cover. She hid her face in her hands and trembled like a sick pup.

On the floor, she lay. She was in fear that, if she looked up, she might find a face from the dark in her view.

Mrs. Hanratty lay there on the cool tile floor, chilled not by what she lay on but by the cold that ran through her veins, until Bobo came to her side and licked her. She went to look up, then she heard one solo gunshot in the night. It was dark; she did not dare move. She heard sirens sound in the distance coming closer.

Chapter Twenty-Two

What a story. Bad cop kills good cop — good cop kills bad. The attorney for the prosecution was bound and determined to find answers in this collaboration of facts and fiction. He did not have full faith in the story the officer had reported and hoped to get to the bottom of it.

"Mrs. Sinclair," said the prosecuting attorney. "Shall we begin?"

Bellamy had prepared herself and de-linked the memories of her past from any psychological response. Softly, in a barely audible voice, she confirmed she was ready.

"Did you know Officer Montoya?"

"Yes, he was the childhood friend of my deceased best friend, and he became my friend." Bellamy thought back, *Jordan, the mess you made. You couldn't keep a promise. So easy to figure out. It came together nicely, like a puzzle. Thank you, friend. You served your purpose well.*

She picked up the attorney's voice again. "Oh, I'm terribly sorry," said Bellamy. "I have a hard time staying focused anymore."

The case was tough enough already. A worst-case scenario. Dirty cop. An embarrassed police department. Cops killing cops. Cops killing the innocent.

A police officer who lost both her grandparents, a career, a home — all that she'd worked hard for. Then, ultimately, her life, so it seemed.

It was just too much to take in, but he didn't want to place the jury further in her lap. He could already feel the case slipping away. After all, Bellamy seemed small and frail and innocent — and was attractive.

"You live in Ustaza?" asked the attorney.

"I did, but I sold my home. I couldn't live in it after what happened inside," Bellamy told the jury. "I currently live elsewhere. I'd rather not say where."

A former police officer, she'd already resigned from the department, citing mental anguish, and was due to receive a substantial settlement.

Bellamy had become an expert in faking two important traits: care and sincerity. She, too, had learned long ago the infinite capacity for looking interested when not. She had long since grown tired of eating the generic brand of macaroni.

She no longer bought into the big lie. Yesterday's values superimposed into today's world. What you campaign for reveals your true motives.

"I understand. Are you able to continue? Please tell the court, in your own words, what happened." The DA, at this point, was just going through the paces.

"As I rushed into the room, Jordan was there with Officer Cerna. I didn't see initially that Jordan had already been shot. He was crouched on the floor." Bellamy sat on the stand, rubbing the stolen worry stone between her fingers.

"Why were the two officers in your house?" asked the attorney.

"Cerna was looking to kill Jordan because Jordan got too close to figuring out how Elaine and her Gichan died," Bellamy lied.

"Is that why he killed Officers Rice and Pasteur?"

"Jordan? No, he couldn't murder a fly. Even if asked, he wouldn't do it. Jordan knew Cerna and others were extorting people and taking bribes. He was afraid they would eventually come after him, like they did to Elaine," Bellamy said, "and me."

"Objection calls for speculation."

"Overruled," said the judge.

"I see," said the attorney, knowing this case was already a lost cause.

"Cerna was dirty and killed Elaine for telling the truth, and Jordan was killed for getting in the way. I had no choice. Cerna had a knife, and he would have killed me too. That's why I had to shoot him," Bellamy said, weaving truths with lies.

"Thank you, Your Honor. I have no further questions," said the attorney.

"The witness is excused," said the judge.

Chapter Twenty-Three

Bellamy's flight landed at the tiny airport. As she walked, she lifted her chin slightly, as though to catch the flowery scent awash through the hall. She passed a tourist on her way out.

"Bonjour."

She ferried her carry-on through the corridor. As she passed under the sign reading "Welcome to Andorra", she looked through the glass partition in the distance and recognized the attractive, tall female leaning against a sports car.

Although she was on the other side of the glass, Bellamy waved. "Hi, Elaine!"

Standing next to her red convertible, parked curbside, Elaine, recognizing Bellamy, threw a two-handed kiss.

Glad she has the top up, Bellamy thought. *May is the wettest month.*

As Elaine pulled the sports car from the curb and headed in the direction of Caldea, she asked, "How did it go?"

"Easy peasy. I hope I was able to help."

"I'm sure Jordan appreciated you. I certainly do. You're a good friend," Elaine said.

"Yeah, I'm sure he's in a good place," Bellamy said.

Elaine detected sarcasm in her voice. "Was any mention made about my Gichan's killer?"

Bellamy turned away, as if to view the passing scenery, not wanting to risk Elaine catching a glimpse of the truth on her face. Bellamy hadn't bothered to follow up because she knew what happened to Gichan.

Gichan was a means to an end. He was used to set a screen. Besides, he was on his way out already anyway. Bellamy momentarily was lost in thought. "They still think it was a suicide."

"No, that's not right. He didn't . . . he wouldn't do that. Someone made it look like a suicide," Elaine said.

To avoid crawling down that gopher hole and tired from the flight, Bellamy miscalculated, taking her fatigue out on Elaine and making things worse. "I got the silly jacket you asked me to," she said.

"You were able to get Jordan's letter jacket back?" Elaine asked.

"Yeah, but why do you bother with it?" Bellamy asked. "Why did you want me to save it?"

Elaine could sense the irritation in Bellamy's tone and facial expression. "When I wear it, I feel like it hugs my memories. It helps me not to forget them."

Shaking her head in disbelief, Bellamy whispered under her breath, loud enough for Elaine to hear, "So stupid."

Jet-lagged or not, Elaine wasn't about to be bullied. She shot back, "You have no right to be jealous of my relationship with Jordan. It's unbecoming."

"I'm not jealous. I just can't figure out what you see in him that was so special."

"He was my first and only love. Jordan's jacket takes me back to a long time ago. When people were kind and different. They made promises and kept them," Elaine said, stealing a glimpse at Bellamy, noticing for the first time that she was rubbing a familiar-looking stone between her fingers.

Bellamy despised that Jordan, even in death, owned Elaine's allegiance — the love that Bellamy believed should be reserved for her was forever his.

She thought for a second, feeling like it was a good time to stab the wounded bear by divulging to Elaine her relationship with Jordan. But instead, she went with, "That reminds me, I ran into a guy at Jordan's memorial service. We had drinks after."

Bellamy held back that, after many whiskeys, she'd invited Christian to her hotel room. She couldn't figure out why Christian had come all the way to her room, only to leave without taking her to bed. He didn't stay long.

"He said his name — Christian. Said he knew you. Felt like he knew me too, in the way he spoke. Made it feel like he was suspicious about what happened," Bellamy said.

Elaine said, "For a long time, he and Jordan have been best friends. He weirdly disappeared off the map. But Jordan mentioned his name a few times."

Remembering back to the time Jordan tossed her his jacket, Elaine knew Christian pushed the buttons to get them together. According to Jordan, Christian was in the military doing "secret squirrel stuff."

She smiled, "He's old school. You can trust and count on him to be a friend." Her expression changed suddenly. "But I would not want to go up against him."

"He gave me his number," Bellamy said.

Elaine, staring silently, straight ahead at the car in front of theirs, finally looked at Bellamy and said, "Did you give him yours?" She gathered there was more to the story than what Bellamy told.

Exasperated, Bellamy raised her voice, "No! Why would I?"

"Around Christian, were you ever not with your phone?"

Bellamy thought back to when Christian was in her hotel room and knew the answer. *When I excused myself to use the ladies' room.*

"No."

Truth be damned, because Elaine had already done the math and figured Christian had already GPS-ed his way to the truth.

"You didn't need to," Elaine said. "He knows now."

Bellamy, sensing Elaine's concern, but without admitting guilt, said, "Don't worry, I got this. When it comes to men, they're all the same. They all think with their other head."

"He and Jordan are different," Elaine said. "Christian plays second fiddle, but he is always running the show."

A gradual sense of foreboding came over Elaine as she negotiated the sports car through town. *This is not over,* she thought.

Epilogue

Elaine sat at a stylish outdoor restaurant that offered a high-end menu with a low-key vibe. She liked it because the seating faced the street, which satisfied the paranoid police officer that she couldn't shake, still living inside her. She heard the muted whistle of a distant train.

"I knew you would come," she said as she stood.

Christian, arms at his sides, did not respond at first, letting Elaine wrap her arms around his neck and shoulders.

"Nine-second hug."

Christian, sensing the same Elaine, obliged her eventually, returning her embrace.

"What can I get you?"

"Iced tea, thanks," he said.

"Iced tea. So you must be here on business," Elaine said.

They talked at first, just catching up on old times. To Elaine, Christian's exploits had only been rumors.

"A secret agent? Was Jordan telling the truth? Are you really a superhero?"

"Jordan always had a way of building things up bigger than they really are," said Christian.

"Somehow, I think he was right," Elaine said. "You always were the one who kicked the bullies off the playground. You liked staying backstage, but you always were the one directing the show."

"I guess you know why I'm here then," Christian said.

"No, why are you really here, Christian? I don't think you're really looking for me."

"I'm not looking for you, Elaine, but I have come looking for the truth."

"I'm sure Jordan told you what they did to me," she said. "They killed Bachan and Gichan. I left right after that. I had to get away before they got me too. There were a lot of loose strings."

"What do you mean?" Christian asked.

"Bellamy ran into Jordan, and he came to help me, and those bastards killed him too. Lucky Bellamy was there. Otherwise, they would have gotten away with dirtying Jordan's name and killing her. Just like they did to me."

"Is that what Bellamy told you?" Christian asked. "What about Amber?"

"Who is Amber?"

"The girl who stood in for you the last day on the playground."

"Christian, you're talking in riddles."

"Bellamy's been lying to you."

Elaine, holding a Cadillac Margarita, stopped mid-drink.

"She killed your grandfather and Amber to cover your exit."

Setting the drink down, Elaine leaned forward, closer to Christian. "What are you saying? You can't be serious! Who told you this?"

"Jordan told me before he was taken off the playground. Bellamy staged all of it. She wanted you all to herself."

The sound in Elaine's ears was deafening. The impact of Christian's words was like bullets ripping through her flesh. "There's no way! Bellamy is a friend! You're wrong."

"She didn't want Jordan hanging around, so she off-ed him too."

"Gichan and Jordan are dead . . . because of me?" Elaine, starting to lose her breath, not wanting to make a scene, removed a folded handkerchief from her purse to cover her mouth.

"Not because of you," Christian said. "They are gone because Cerna and the others were dirty. Bellamy is dirty too."

"That bitch!" Elaine blurted out the words, realizing by the nearby reactions that she was too loud. "How could she do this?"

"Your problem is you trust people. In school, we always believed people were good. You and Jordan stayed the same. Somewhere along the way, I changed," Christian said, determining that Elaine's rage was real.

After a moment, Elaine, afraid of the answer, asked, "What comes next?"

"Maybe you should go back home."

"To what and do what? Christian, I have no home."

"Okay, Elaine," he said, "You do you, and I'll do me."

As Christian stood from the table, Elaine grabbed his arm and handed him the worry stone Jordan had given her so many years before. "Nine-second hug?"

After Christian let go, he kissed her lightly on the forehead.

"I know who has the other one," Elaine said.

Handing the stone back, Christian said, "You keep this one. I don't worry much anymore. I'm the one who makes others worry."

"Do I have anything to worry about?" Elaine said.

"I'm still your friend."

"Will I ever see you again?"

"Who knows? Never say never. Take care of yourself."

Elaine stood and thought as she watched Christian walk away, *Bellamy, it is about to get very ugly for you.*